Sarah Lean's fascination with animals began when she was aged eight and a stray cat walked in the back door and decided to adopt her. As a child she wanted to be a writer and used to dictate stories to her mother, until she bought a laptop of her own several years ago and decided to type them herself. She loves her garden, art, calligraphy and spending time outdoors. She lives in Dorset and shares the space around her desk with her dogs, Harry and Coco.

www.sarahlean.co.uk

Also by Sarah Lean

A Dog Called Homeless

Winner of the Hazelgrove Book Award
and the prestigious Schneider Middle School
Book Award in the US.
Shortlisted for the Sheffield Children's Book
Award and longlisted for the
Branford Boase Award.

Hero

Shortlisted for the
Coventry Inspiration Book Awards.

A Horse for Angel

The Forever Whale

Jack Pepper

Praise for Sarah Lean

"Sarah Lean weaves magic and emotion into beautiful stories." *Cathy Cassidy*

"Touching, reflective and lyrical." *The Sunday Times*

"… beautifully written and moving. A talent to watch." *The Bookseller*

"Sarah Lean's graceful, miraculous writing will have you weeping one moment and rejoicing the next." Katherine Applegate, author of *The One and Only Ivan*

SARAH LEAN

Harry and Hope

Illustrated by Gary Blythe

HarperCollins *Children's Books*

First published in Great Britain by HarperCollins *Children's Books* in 2015
HarperCollins *Children's Books* is a division of HarperCollins*Publishers* Ltd,
1 London Bridge Street, London, SE1 9GF

The HarperCollins website address is: www.harpercollins.co.uk

1

ISBN 978-0-00-751226-3

Printed and bound in England by Clays Ltd, St Ives plc

FSC™ is a non-profit international organisation established to promote
the responsible management of the world's forests. Products carrying the
FSC label are independently certified to assure consumers that they come
from forests that are managed to meet the social, economic and
ecological needs of present and future generations,
and other controlled sources.

Find out more about HarperCollins and the environment at
www.harpercollins.co.uk/green

For my little sister

1.

IT MUST HAVE SNOWED ON THE MOUNTAIN IN the night.

"Have you seen it yet, Frank?" I shouted downstairs.

"You mean did I hear?"

"I know, funny, isn't it? The snow's so quiet but it's making all the animals noisy."

We didn't normally see snow on Canigou in May,

and it made the village dogs bark in that crazy way dogs do when something is out of place. Harry, Frank's donkey, was down in his shed, chin up on the half open door, calling like a creaky violin.

Frank came up to the roof terrace where I'd been sleeping in the hammock. He leaned over the red tiles next to me and we looked at Canigou, sparkling at the top like a jewellery shop.

And it's the kind of thing that is hard to describe, when snow is what you can see while the sun is warming your skin. How did it feel? To see one thing and feel the complete opposite? I only knew that other things didn't seem to fit together properly at the moment either; that my mother and Frank seemed as far apart as the snow and the sun.

"Frank, at school Madame was telling us that

the things we do affect the environment, you know, like leaving lights on, things like that," I said. "Well, I left the lights on in the girls' loo."

Frank smiled. Frank was my mother's boyfriend, but that won't tell you what he meant to me at all. He'd lived in our guesthouse next door for three years and he wouldn't ever say the things to me that Madame had said when I forgot to turn the lights off. In fact, what he did was leave a soft friendly silence, so I knew I could ask what I wanted to ask, because I wasn't sure about the whole environment thing.

"Did I make it snow on Canigou?"

"Leave the light on and see if it snows again," he whispered, grinning.

He made the world seem real simple, like a little light switch right under my fingertips. But there were other complicated things.

"Remember when the cherry blossom fell a few weeks ago?" I said.

He nodded.

"How many people do you think have seen pink snow?"

"Only people who see the world like you."

"And you."

I looked out from all four corners of the terrace.

South was the meadow, and then the Massimos' vineyards that belonged to my best friend Peter's family – lines and lines of vines curving over the steep mountainside, making long lazy shadows across the red soil paths. I thought of the vines with their new green leaves twirling along the gnarly arms, reaching out to curl around each other, like they needed to know they weren't alone; that they'd be strong enough together to grow their grapes.

North were the gigantic plane trees with big

roots and trunks that cracked the roads and pavements around the village.

East was the village, the roofs of the houses stacked on the mountainside like giant orangey coloured books left open and abandoned halfway through a story.

West were the cherry fields, and Canigou, the highest peak that we could see in the French Pyrenees. It soared over the village and the vineyards, high above us.

I touched the things I kept in the curve of the roof tiles, the wooden things Frank had carved for me. I whispered their names and picked them up, familiar, warm and softly smooth in my hands: humming bird, the letter H, mermaid, donkey, cherries, and the latest one – the olive tree knot made into a walking-stick handle that Frank said I might need to lean on to go around the vineyards with Peter when we're ninety-nine. Always in that order. The order that Frank made them.

"What you thinking about, Frank?"

"The world," he said quietly. "And cherry blossom."

When you're twelve, it takes a long time for the different sounds and words you've heard and the things you've seen to end up some place deep inside of you where you can make sense of them. It was that morning when I worked out what my feelings had been trying to tell me; when I saw Frank looking at our mountain like he was remembering something he missed; when I saw the passport sticking out of his pocket.

It felt like even the crazy dogs had known before me, as if even the mountain had been listening and watching and trying to tell me.

Frank looked over.

"Spill," he said, which is what he always said when he knew there were words swirling inside me that I couldn't seem to get out.

"Why did you travel all around the world, Frank? I mean, you went to loads of different countries for twenty years before you came here, and that's, like, a really, really long time to be travelling."

"Something in me," he said.

"But you don't need to go travelling again, do you?"

For three whole years my mother and I had been more than the rest of the world to him.

He looked down at his pocket, knew what I had seen. Tilted his leather hat forward to shade his eyes.

"What I mean is..." I didn't know exactly how to explain. A boyfriend was somebody for my mother. For me, it used to be a person who picked me up and swirled me around and bought me soft toys which, after a while, I binned because the person who bought them always left. But that wasn't what Frank did. There wasn't a word for what Frank was to me. I mean, how can you explain something when there isn't even a word for it? I just wanted to ask: if he was thinking about leaving, what about me? How would we still fit together?

"What I mean is..." I tried again. "Say you like cherries, which I do, and then you eat them with almonds, which I also like a lot... you get something else, right? Something that makes the cherries more cherry-ish and the almonds more kind of almond-y."

"Like tomatoes and basil?" Frank said. His favourite.

Down below us, Harry kicked at his door. And

Harry… well, you couldn't have Frank without Harry. They were definitely as good together as yoghurt and honey.

"Yes, like that," I said. "But also you and Harry, Mum and you, you know, there's these kinds of pairs of us."

"You and Peter?"

"Yeah, us too. These pairs you made of us." I picked the little wooden donkey up, turned it in my hands. "I feel kind of smoother, and sort of… *more*, when we're together." That's what I felt about me and Frank. "I'm kind of *more me* when you're around."

"Hope Malone," he said. "You have your own things that are just you."

I said, "But I'd be just half of me without you."

Frank pushed his passport deeper into his pocket.

"Are you planning on going somewhere, Frank?"

"We'll talk later," he said as Harry's hoof clattered against his shed again. "I'd better let that donkey out before he kicks the door down."

2.

ANYBODY WOULD LOVE HARRY STRAIGHT AWAY. As soon as you put your hand out to touch him and he greeted you in his nuzzly donkey kind of way, he made you feel so nice. He was only little, about as high as my waist, with stick spindly legs, but round where there was much more of him in the middle. I always thought he was a bit shy, the way his eyelashes curled up and the fact that he never looked you in the eye. He seemed to hear everything Frank said, though, like the words poured down his tall ears and into his whole skin and bones and barrelled belly.

"Going somewhere?" Frank said, as Harry barged out of his shed, quivering with happiness just because Frank spoke to him. Harry trotted straight over to the trailer hitched to the back of Frank's dusty jeep.

"Where are you going?" I asked.

"Same as always," Frank said.

I mean, I knew where they were going because they always did the same thing every day. Frank would have to drive Harry along the lane and back again before Harry would go down to the meadow. It was an old habit of Harry's from their travelling days years ago. If they didn't go for a spin with the jeep and trailer, Harry wouldn't go down to the meadow, no matter how big the carrot you held in front of his nose was. I completely got it, why Harry had to have things as they always were. Frank had rescued Harry and brought him over from India. Harry was safe, getting in the trailer every day and not going back to how his awful life was.

Same as always. But what about Frank's passport?

I watched them go before running back up to the roof to get dressed.

Marianne was up there with her camera, taking photographs of Canigou.

Everyone called my mother Marianne, even me most of the time. She was an artist. Her bedroom and studio, where she'd normally be, were on the first floor next to each other. She usually stayed there most of the day and didn't come out into the world if she didn't want to. We weren't allowed to go and disturb her either.

"The cherry blossom's all gone," she said.

"It's been gone ages."

"Oh, I hadn't noticed."

I coughed. "Excuse me, I want to get dressed."

"I'm not looking," she said, turning the camera towards Canigou. "Why are you sleeping up here anyway?"

As soon as it was warm enough I had wanted to sleep outside, so that if I woke up, I would see the dark shape of the mountain between the stars, even on the blackest night. I didn't say that though, because I couldn't talk to her about things like that. I couldn't have just burst into her space and told her that the blossom was falling and it was so beautiful I might explode. There's only that one moment when you feel like that and then it's gone, and these things I wanted to say didn't ever seem to fit with Marianne at the right time. So I'd gone and told Frank and he'd stood and watched with me and there was nothing left to say anyway, because Frank and I were the same, all filled up with that blustery breeze making pink snow of the blossom.

"It's too hot in my bedroom," I said, rummaging under the blankets drooping over the hammock and on to the floor. "I can't find my shoes."

"Where are the new ones I bought you?"

I shrugged.

"In your other bedroom, probably still in the box," said Marianne.

I took my clothes downstairs and got changed. I grabbed my new shoes from the box in my room and a croissant from the kitchen and went outside with the croissant in my mouth to wait for Harry and Frank.

When they got back, Harry trotted out of the

trailer, looked around, and Frank frowned and said to him, "You never give up, do you, Harry?"

"He's a creature of habit," I said. The croissant muffled the words in my mouth and flakes dropped all over me so I jumped up and down to shake them off. "That's what you always say. Like all of us."

"Seen Marianne this morning?" Frank asked.

I nodded. "I expect she's in her studio now."

I shoved my feet in my shoes without pushing my heels in and scuffed after Frank and Harry. Slowly Harry headed to the meadow, as always, in that kind of, *oh yeah, I nearly forgot, there's a lovely meadow for me here* kind of way. I hoped Frank still thought that too. That this was the place where they both fitted perfectly.

Frank pointed towards something lying in the grass. I'd left my other shoes in the meadow yesterday. Harry had chewed on them. Frank had made me lots of rules since he lived here. Marianne said artists don't like rules. But I'd got used to Frank's because he was never mean and bossy, and that helped me remember them, almost all the time.

"Oh," I said, picking the shoes up, disappointed I'd done something stupid. The canvas was shredded, the laces unravelled. "I know, I know, I'm not supposed to leave anything in the meadow. Sorry, it was just this one time I forgot because Peter and I were hiding things in the grass and trying to find them with bare feet and our eyes closed. I won't do it again."

"Hope—"

"I don't mind, honest. I've got these," I lifted my foot up to show Frank the new ones and hooked the back with a finger to get my heel in.

"The others were too small anyway."

"What might happen to Harry if he ate something he shouldn't?"

"Oh." But Frank didn't make me feel stupid, just kind of like I'd try harder next time. "Sorry. Sorry, Harry."

Frank shoved his hands in his pockets and I followed his eyes to the snow on Canigou. I hadn't finished what I was saying earlier.

"Do you think it works the other way around?" I said. "I mean, because of the environment, because Canigou is different today, can it change us?"

Frank had stayed put for three years now. Had he changed enough to stay for good?

I looked across and Frank didn't say anything because we had this other kind of quiet world where we totally got each other. He taught me you didn't always have to have an answer straight away.

"Where you off to today?" he said instead.

"I *was* going to the waterfall," I said, cramming the last of the croissant into my mouth. "Peter and I were going to check on the swing to see if it needs fixing, ready for summer holidays. But actually I think I'll stay here today. With you and Harry."

"Peter's last day, isn't it?" Peter went to boarding school in England and was only home for the break.

"Yes, but—"

"Go on," Frank said. "I'll be here when you get back."

I still didn't go.

"I'll find some wood." He smiled.

I knew that meant we'd sit outside by the fire-pit

this evening, talking in the honey-coloured light with the mountain looking over us. About all the things I couldn't say to Marianne.

All I had to do was find a way to remind Frank of all the good things about being here, all the good things that made pairs of us, and then he wouldn't even think about going anywhere else.

I nodded.

"See you by the fire later," he said.

3.

Before I met Peter, I'd only ever heard that he was the rich kid from the vineyards and didn't play with anyone else in the village, which was enough information for me to think we'd never be friends. The day that Frank and Harry arrived three years ago, Peter turned up too. He sat on the meadow fence and watched Frank introducing me to Harry, and then all Peter did was come over and ask Frank if he could stroke Harry too.

Frank said what he'd already just said to me when I'd asked the *exact* same question. "You need to give Harry a bit of time to get used to you first." I looked at Peter's big brown eyes, and when Frank said, "He doesn't know yet if you're going to be kind to him," I murmured along with Frank what I knew he was going to say next: "even though I do."

I had one more day with Peter before I lost him to boarding school and would have to wait ages for him to be on holiday again. I ran across the meadow and Harry trotted alongside me until I climbed through the hole in the fence, into the vineyard, and raced on to Peter's grandparents' house, turning back to see Harry with his chin up on the top rung, his ears pointing high, watching me go.

"See you later, Harry!"

That donkey would always think he was coming with you.

Peter was dressed smart, as always. Even if we were going crawling through vineyards or driving Monsieur Vilaro's rusty old tractor he looked kind of pressed and tidy and new. I liked my clothes, they made me feel comfortably like me, but I always got the feeling when I was next to Peter that actually my clothes were scruffy, not casual.

Peter was packing a towel into a bag.

"Are you going swimming? We never swim until July. The water's too cold," I said. "And anyway I haven't brought a towel."

"I'm going to swim; you can watch. If you change your mind then you can share my towel."

"I thought we were going to make the swing ready for when you come back?"

"We are," he said, winking. "Ciao, Nanu," (which means *Bye, Nanny*) he called back as I followed him outside. Peter's grandparents were Italian and although they'd lived here in France for over fifty years, they still didn't speak much French or English, unlike Peter.

Outside, Peter said, all kind of secretive, "Today's the day."

"The day for what?"

"Jumping off the waterfall."

"You say that every year."

"I mean it this time."

"What, from the top? You've always said it's too high."

"But I'm taller than I was before."

I looked at the top of his head. With my hand,

I measured his height against me, pressing his thick wavy hair down in case that was what was making him look taller, but he'd had his hair cut short ready for school, so it wasn't that.

"For the first time ever, you are actually just a teeny, weeny bit taller than me," I said, which made him grin. "But *I'm* not doing it."

As we walked we discussed the good and bad things about jumping off waterfalls, asking each other if we'd heard of Angel Falls and Victoria Falls, Peter agreeing in the end that he would swim to the bottom first to check if there were any rocks under the water.

There was a shortcut across the Vilaros' field, although we weren't supposed to use it, and when we got near the gate the Vilaros' guard dog, Bruno, blocked our way. Bruno usually just paced around the field, guarding against… well, I had no idea what, but this time he barked and barked at us in that way that made you not want to go any further.

Bruno's chops dripped drool with the effort of the big noise he was making and Peter turned and walked back down the lane (well, kind of ran actually), probably expecting me to be right behind him as usual. Bruno was a big dog, not a house dog, with battle-tatty ears and grey chops, and I'd never taken much notice of him before, except when I had to avoid him on the way to school, but there was something about him that day that I couldn't ignore.

"All right, Bruno, we're not going across the field," I said.

He kept barking, to tell me he was on patrol and wouldn't be letting us past.

"Hope, come on! We can go through the vineyards instead," Peter called.

All the dogs in the village were crazy with something that day and although Bruno was usually barky and grumpy, he seemed more upset than usual.

"Peter, I think something's wrong."

"Come away. Bruno doesn't look very happy about us being here."

"He's never bitten us before."

"That doesn't mean he won't today."

"Peter, wait. I can't just leave him on his own like this."

In my pocket were some sherbet lemons. I thought if I gave Bruno something sweet it might make him stop barking and howling like that. I threw one at him and he snatched it up and spat it out again, probably because when you think about it lemons aren't that sweet at all. He kept barking, looking at Peter and me, then staring up at the mountain.

"Look, Peter. Bruno isn't even barking at us. He's barking at the snow."

Peter peeked out from behind the hedge at the bottom of the lane, his eyes wide when he realised I wasn't with him, madly waving me to come.

"Bruno?" I said. "Are you talking about the mountain?"

Bruno watched Peter creeping back up the lane on tiptoes, all hunched up and clinging to the hedge, whispering, "Hope! Please come!"

"Peter, you're being silly," I said, "Bruno isn't going to hurt us. I think he might even be trying to talk *to* Canigou, and he has to bark big and loud like that so it can hear."

Peter rolled his eyes at me, which he does a lot, and said, "Now who's being silly? Let's go!"

By now Peter had crept back to where I was. He grabbed my hand and then I was running with him down the lane in that way, you know, when you feel like you're not going to stop and it makes you excited and scared at the same time, and you scream and laugh together, and it felt good so I didn't look back at that big old barky dog.

Peter and I climbed over the vineyard fence and through the hole in the hedge, a hole we'd made for avoiding Bruno before. We ran up the long path of stony earth between the vines, turned right to go through the next vineyard, and then across the track behind the Vilaros' field. Bruno had raced through the field up to the wall and was still barking, his paws up on the wall, and then suddenly he stopped. Everything went silent. After all that noise, it made me look up instead of where my feet had to go.

"Peter!" I pointed, because I didn't know how

to say what I was seeing, although what I felt like saying was: *The mountain answered Bruno.*

It seemed to me like Canigou was a giant that had been asleep for a long time, breathing slowly, very slowly. And then maybe what happened was that the cold of the new snow was too heavy, too wintry and unexpected, and the mountain had to shift a bit to get comfortable again. And that made the avalanche happen.

A huge chunk of snow was falling down the mountainside, making a big white billowy mist, as if it was turning back into a cloud of snowflakes again. Even from where we were, the rumble of the fall and the crack of snapped trees echoed across to us as the avalanche slid down.

Peter moved in front of me. He knew as well as I did that the snow was too far away and would never reach us – that we were safe – but looking out for me was the kind of thing that Peter did.

We stood there for a long time watching the snow roll and tumble, until at last everything stopped and was quiet again. Even the insects had stopped buzzing and the leaves had stopped shuffling. It was now really, really quiet.

"The mountain shrugged," I whispered, because that was what it seemed like to me.

Peter rolled his eyes again. "The world according to Hope Malone," he said, like he usually did.

People appeared; Monsieur Vilaro on his tractor and some people who worked in the vineyards, running up the slopes with Peter's grandfather, Nonno, all heading towards the edge of the spilt snow.

Nonno saw us and came jogging over, his bandy legs making him lurch side to side. He wiped the sweat from his forehead, spoke to Peter in Italian, before swaying back to the men all gathering together.

"Nonno said we should go home," Peter translated. "To stay out of the way, just in case another avalanche happens."

We didn't go, not straight away, even though Peter was pestering me to leave, to do as we were told.

"Can you feel it, Peter?" I whispered.

"The snow?"

"I don't know. Something like that. I can smell it too."

I held out my arms to see if the air felt different on my skin.

"It seems the same to me," Peter said.

We went back the way we came, through the vineyards towards my house, and I saw our footprints from where we'd walked earlier, where the red earth was softest, exactly as we'd left them.

Everything was about to change though, and, like the avalanche, there was nothing I could do to stop it.

4.

"Frank! Where are you?" I called, as Peter and I ran up the drive.

Harry came first, trotting up from the meadow to see what was going on. The meadow had fences on three sides, except the top side next to the gravel drive, although Harry usually acted as if there was one there and didn't stray out.

There were old rotting planks of wood stacked outside the guesthouse, and the guesthouse door was open. Frank came out.

"There was an avalanche on Canigou!" I said, with the little breath I had left.

"You OK?" said Frank, pulling me close.

I nodded against his chest.

Frank held me away and looked into my face. "How far did the snow come down?"

"As far as the casot," Peter said. "You know, the old shepherd's hut?"

"Has anybody else gone up there yet?"

"Nonno's there and a few others."

"I'll take the top road in the jeep, see if there's anything I can do. Hope, tell your mother where I'm going."

Frank, as he always was. Frank to the rescue.

He ran to the jeep and Harry followed him.

“Not this time,” Frank called to Harry. “Keep hold of him, Hope!”

Harry tried to go after him. Peter and I held on as best we could, our feet skidding in the dust as Harry dragged us along for a bit. Even though he was little, with short thin legs, he was really, really strong. Harry couldn’t help himself, he always wanted to go with Frank if Frank was going anywhere.

As the jeep sped off, Harry watched the dust spitting up behind, his ears leaning right forward as if they were still following the sound of Frank leaving.

“Come on, Harry,” I said. “Back to the meadow.”

It was easy to say that to him, but Frank was the only one who could get Harry to do what he wanted.

I got carrots from the kitchen to try to lead

him down there, but he stood there for ages, not moving, no matter what Peter and I said.

Sometimes I wasn't sure how much Harry understood, although he seemed to completely understand Frank. Even though Frank didn't say much to him, there was a whole world of things that they said to each other without words. Other times, I thought Harry was just thinking like a donkey has to think: about all the fresh grass at his feet and how much he could eat before going in his shed for the night.

Harry wouldn't look me in the eye, but then again he never did. Not even with Frank. In fact, Harry always looked kind of sad, and that was probably because of the way his head drooped as if there was something heavy on his mind.

The words to describe Frank and Harry are those that anybody would understand: best mates.

The best way to describe what Frank was to me is like this:

One day a man (I forget who) came over to our house to see Frank about getting some carpentry work done. I was outside and so was Frank, who was painting the shutters, and the man said hello to me first, and then he saw Frank climbing down from the ladder and said, "Can I speak to your dad?"

And I said, "He's not my dad, he's my..." and couldn't finish what I was saying, even though that wasn't what the man thought was important right then. My mouth was still open, ready to say a word that fitted exactly right after 'my', but Frank was already striding over holding out his big brown Australian hand, which had paint on it, and he wiped it on his jeans first and said, "I'm Frank, what can I do for ya, mate?"

Marianne told me my father was an art dealer. I'd never met him so I didn't miss him because I didn't know him or what there was to miss. He didn't fit with us and I suppose we didn't fit with him either, so I was OK with that. But me and Frank, we'd never filled in the blank about who we were to each other.

It took ages for Peter and me to get Harry to go to the meadow. In the end, I think he made up his own mind to go.

Peter and I wandered back to the house talking about what we thought everyone might be doing up at the avalanche and I noticed that Frank had left his door open. I wasn't ever supposed to go in without knocking and never had, but I was sure he hadn't meant to leave it open.

As I closed the door, through the gap I saw a pile of clothes on Frank's bed.

For a minute, something like that makes your mind do all sorts of things. Like adding things up. Passport, half-packed bag and… what else? Just a kind of uncomfortable feeling.

I ran up to the roof.

"Where are you going?" Peter said, running up after me.

"To see."

Because of the plane trees, we couldn't see the casot or where the snow had fallen from there. Most of the land belonged to the Massimos and Peter was quiet until he said, "Where the snow fell, that was where the new vineyard had been planted."

I wanted to feel something about what he said, but I couldn't. I wanted to see something else other than Frank's travelling bag and the passport in his pocket.

5.

When Frank arrived home later, Harry headed straight back up from the meadow and went over to the jeep, walked all the way around it and then followed Frank.

I hung back.

"Was anyone hurt?" Peter asked, running up to him.

"The casot helped stop the avalanche," Frank

said. "The snow's wedged up behind it. It's smashed up a bit but it looks like nobody was up there."

"It doesn't matter about the casot; nobody's used it for about fifty years," said Peter.

"The new vineyard… it's under the snow too," said Frank softly.

Peter's shoulders dropped. His family wanted to make more wine and more money, give more people jobs. The soil and the sun and the vines and the Massimos all fitted together perfectly up here too.

"New things will grow," Frank said. "They always do."

"Was Nonno OK?" Peter said. "He gets tired easily."

Frank smiled at Peter and touched his shoulder. "I gave him a lift home."

"I'd better go back. I want to see him."

"Peter! Will I see you before you go?" I said.

"Ciao, Hope! See you in the summer," Peter called as he ran.

"Family comes first, hey?" Frank said.

I was still standing on the porch not knowing what to say.

"Frank?" I caught his sleeve and asked him. "Are you going somewhere?"

Moments passed while he seemed to measure out the right amount of words to say, while I hooked my fingers together around his arm.

At last, he said, "Nonno has asked me to help with digging out some of the vines and posts from the snow, see what we can salvage of the new vineyard. Might take weeks, or more."

"You're not going anywhere else?"

"Like I said, I'm needed here."

Had Frank been about to leave? If it hadn't been for the avalanche... I looked back at Canigou. I knew I had always been right about my giant friend: that it stood by me, no matter what.

"Come and help me light the fire," Frank said. "We still got some talking to do."

My mother turned out the lights in her studio upstairs, which meant that Frank, Harry and I were the brightest things on the hillside, made amber by our fire.

Frank went inside and brought out some papers to throw on the fire, and we collected up the old rotting bits of wood that he'd been sorting out earlier to burn. I leaned on him, hooked one leg over his so he knew I wanted to sit in his lap.

"You're really comfortable to sit on, Frank."

"You're getting kinda big," he said after a while.

"I'm not heavy though, am I?"

He laughed. "Big on the inside."

I sat on a shorter log next to him.

"I'm cold now," I said.

He gave me his sheepskin jacket. Sheep were the warmest creatures, he'd once said, and he thought it was mad that millions of them lived in the sweltering heat in Australia, which was where Frank was born. Wrapped in his jacket was kind of like being Frank, or at least part of him, smelling of fire smoke and the outside and long journeys.

I leaned my head against his side. Harry came over and blinked from the heat of the fire.

Frank threw old papers into the flames. The little burning pieces shot into the sky and made us our own kind of fluttering stars. Flakes of the burnt papers fell towards me as they died in the sky. I caught one and it made a soft grey mark on my palm.

"We gonna talk?" Frank nudged me and I didn't answer for a while, probably like him, weighing up what I did and didn't want to say.

"I've been thinking," he said. It wasn't like him to go first. It was usually me spilling over with questions. "What you said earlier about cherries."

"I'm right, aren't I?" I smiled into the fire.

"I get it."

"I know. I never knew anyone before like you or Harry."

We were both quiet again after that.

Everything turned to shadows when the sun fell behind Canigou, making the sky bright blue around our mountain's shoulders. I had a different feeling, of being held up like a piece of washing on a line by a flimsy wooden peg.

"Spill," Frank whispered.

Perhaps it had always been hard for him too. I wanted Frank to understand what I didn't know how to say. That even if my mother and he didn't want to be together, that somehow we'd still be each half of a pair, even if there wasn't a word for us.

The only reason we'd all come together in the first place was because of Harry. Harry's life hadn't all been happy, but if it wasn't for that donkey, none of us would ever have met.

I nudged Frank and he squinted one eye in that here-we-go-again kind of way but with an added ton of patience, because he knew what I wanted to hear.

"You want me to tell you again how I found Harry?" he said.

"From the beginning."

6.

FRANK HADN'T EXACTLY TOLD ME THE STORY OF Harry, not like someone normally tells you a story, by starting at the beginning, going on to the middle and then ending at the end. You had to prise bits of it out of him, ask questions, even the same ones again and again, and then sometimes he'd let a bit more spill. But the end of the story was always the same. They ended up here.

Sometimes Frank talked about 'the grey donkey' rather than Harry. I thought maybe he was protecting Harry by not calling him by his name when he spoke about where he came from. Or maybe it was so Harry wouldn't hear. Like I said, you never can tell how much a donkey understands.

Actually, I hated the story, because of what had happened to Harry, but I loved it too. Because of Frank.

"Fire away," he said, like always, and we both smiled because the bonfire and the talk had always gone together.

"How did you find Harry?" I began.

Frank took a big breath, like he was preparing himself deep down inside. He picked two sappy grasses, held one out to me, getting ready to go travelling in his memory and take me with him.

"Paths crossed, I reckon."

"Where was it you were going?"

"Travelling, that's all."

"But, like, where were you exactly?"

"India, Mumbai, near a building site."

"And what were you doing at the building site?"

"Just looking, watching things change."

"What made you stop for Harry?"

He shook his head and twitched his lip as he crushed the grass stem between his teeth.

"There are some things that a man finds hard to pass by."

I loved the way he talked. Bold and sure. Each time the answers familiar, but that day, strangely unfamiliar too. Maybe that was because of me hearing them differently, because I had grown since the last time he'd told me the story. Or maybe it was because something cold had settled in my stomach, like a sprinkling of snow.

"How big was the pile of bricks Harry was carrying?" I asked.

"Bigger than himself."

"He was a good donkey though," I said, knowing the story so well.

Frank nodded.

"So why did his owner treat him like he did?"

Again he waited a moment, leaving a space, like that silence was the place for me to work things out, to be ready to see the things he'd seen.

Frank threw the last of his papers on the fire. New sparks rose.

"When the donkey fell, the man couldn't see that he'd have got up if he could."

"What did you do, Frank?"

He poked the ashes with a stick.

"Pulled him back on his feet."

I didn't ask any more about this part of the

story, eager to get past the struggle that I couldn't bear to hear. Frank had never given any details, as if he was saving poor Harry from being shamed by what happened. And I kind of understood, if you can call it understanding by putting your own thoughts in a donkey's head. Harry was strong and willing and he would have got up if he could, but Frank had to help him.

"You wanted to carry some of the bricks for Harry," I reminded Frank.

He studied the crushed stem he'd been chewing. It took him a long time to answer and I wondered if there was another bit missing, a bit that Frank didn't tell me.

"I made it worse. Poor grey donkey," Frank said. I never understood this. How could anything be worse than poor Harry almost buried under his load? But Frank said no more. I wondered if he did it on purpose, stopping right at that point to give his story just about as much weight as Harry's burden of bricks, to let the fact of the story sit inside me for a while so I could feel how heavy his heart had been when he'd seen the grey donkey buckling and having no choice but to try to get up and carry on.

"But you *saved* Harry! You bought him and took him away and he's never had to work hard like that again."

Frank rested his cheeks on his fists. He'd gone quiet. I knew the story so well I filled in the rest for him. The good bit.

"You rescued Harry. Together you travelled across countries that I've never even heard of, your tyres popping all the time while you drove up those stony mountain roads, following your friends from Germany who were on their motorbikes and who had maps of how to get to Europe. Then they helped you get visas and papers, to have all the checks that you and Harry had to have."

I followed Frank's eyes to the bonfire, to the papers now burning at our feet.

"And you avoided all the places where people would ask you too many questions about Harry, and all the time he was safe in the trailer behind your jeep with a pile of straw and a bunch of carrots."

I could feel the freedom they must have had, travelling along like that together.

Frank looked over at me and I couldn't help that the smoke from the fire was getting in my eyes.

"Then he had to go into quarantine. You hated that bit, being without Harry. I would too."

"Listen," Frank said. "Like I said, I've been

thinking—" but I didn't want to hear. I didn't want any of the words to be things I didn't want him to say. I hadn't meant to remind him that he loved travelling but I couldn't hold things in any longer. If Frank left, and Harry with him, I didn't know what I'd do.

"So have I," I said, wedged up against him. "And right now it feels like only a minute ago that you and Harry arrived. And I feel the same, exactly the same as I did when I first met you and Harry."

He rested his head on mine. I kept going.

"Remember when you came? All the dust your jeep kicked up, making big sandy dust flowers blooming along the lane all at once. Like all of a sudden everything was ready for you. Or we were. And I know you didn't say yes at first..." I pulled Harry closer so Frank and Harry made a sandwich around me. "I remember you stood there for the longest time at the edge of the meadow and Marianne said there was no reason a donkey couldn't live here because nobody used it. And you talked to Harry and I wish I knew what you'd said to him. Was it you or Harry who decided to stay?"

Frank laughed softly.

"Harry."

"Harry?! See, he knew this place was right for you. Freshest greenest meadow he'd ever seen in his life, that's what you always say. And I said I'll brush him for you, he looks kind of grey, and you said..."

"He's grey underneath that dust too."

We smiled at Harry, his head and eyes drooping with sleep, standing quietly beside me. We touched him gently and I knew it was impossible for either of us ever to be without him. Harry chose the meadow, and that put me and Frank together too.

"You tell the story of Harry better than I ever did," Frank said.

"He's like the reason for all of us being together, Frank."

I hoped that made sense to him and I think it did because he smiled in that way that made me feel even the whole world had nothing like we had.

He spoke to Harry, like I was supposed to hear too.

"What are we gonna do about you, Harry? You've still got some bad old habits, mate, and it's just not good for you. I think we've gotten too used to each other and I'm not sure I can help you break them any more."

Sometimes you want to show someone that there's a good reason why you're together too.

"I could help," I said. "I mean, like you said, I am growing up and I love Harry. I could help him."

Frank leaned over to Harry and patted his neck, slowly running his hand down Harry's nose, having the kind of conversation that only they could have without saying any words. Then Frank said to him, "What do you reckon, Harry? Do you trust Hope? Me too."

"Really? I'll train Harry?"

"That's what I've been thinking. Nobody knows Harry like I do. It's about time I let you in on that."

"What, like, me look after him? Me and Harry?" Beautiful, sweet, safe Harry.

"How about we start now."

7.

"SEE IF YOU CAN PUT HARRY IN FOR THE NIGHT," Frank said.

"What do I do?"

"Wait here a second." He strode ahead over to the bench outside the guesthouse and sat down. I guessed he was getting out of the way so that Harry and I could do this together by ourselves.

He called, "Tap his shoulder twice, left shoulder, and he'll follow."

I'd seen Frank do it a thousand times, but it's not the same when you do it yourself and you haven't realised it has to be his left shoulder and your fingers are nervous. Harry curved his neck around and looked at my hand. Like we didn't speak the same language, not yet anyway.

"Come on, Harry," I said, and started to walk. He didn't follow.

I went back and did it again and Harry looked at my hand again, and I told him again, "Harry, come on, time to go inside."

Harry looked over at Frank, one ear up, one ear down. He stayed where he was.

"Does he only understand Indian?" I said, which I realised was stupid as I'd never heard Frank use any other language.

Frank laughed. "It's not the words or your voice he's listening to. You have to feel that you mean it, so he feels it too. Feel sure. Then he'll be part of you."

Frank was about to get up and come back over. Of course that was what I wanted. Me and Harry, Me and Frank.

"Yes! I can do it. Give me a minute."

Frank sat back down.

"And I was only joking," I called over. "About talking Indian, I mean."

"Take your time. He'll be ready when you are." Frank leaned back, rested one ankle on the other knee, his arm stretched across the back of the bench.

I stood beside Harry, tidied his fringe. I didn't want to disappoint anybody, including myself. I knew there was something between Harry and me that I had to find – what Frank and Harry had, what Peter and I had. When you just kind of fall in with each other's footsteps.

I looked over at Frank.

If I looked after Harry, would I be completely in their world? Would that make it impossible for me and Frank and Harry to ever be apart? It was all I wanted. I'd never wanted anything so much, or tried so hard.

I thought of me and Harry. Of us being like yoghurt and honey too. I tapped Harry on his left shoulder twice. This time, he followed.

I couldn't stop smiling at the little grey donkey, who was with me in a way he'd never been before. It felt huge and new and exciting.

When Harry got closer to his shed, he went over to see Frank. Maybe Harry was just checking they were still best mates, or maybe he wanted to tell Frank in his nuzzly donkey kind of way that he was OK with the choice he'd made for me to look after him too.

Frank sat forward, wrists dangling over his knees.

"Good boy, Harry," he said.

Harry leaned his head over Frank's shoulder. They said something else to each other again, but not in words or a language I understood, yet.

"Has he got clean water?" Frank said.

I checked inside the shed and ran back to tell him, "I filled the bucket up, right to the top. And changed the bedding."

Frank patted Harry, just like he always did. I loved that about Frank, how he changed things without anyone being left out.

"G'night, Harry, mate," he said. Magic words.

Harry turned away and I took him into the

shed, fresh with straw and an apple I'd left for him to chomp on.

Something nearly broke and fell in pieces that day. But now I was completely in their world, somehow more part of Frank and Harry than ever before.

8.

THE SNOW MELTED.

Frank drove me over to see the broken casot, where the wall had fallen in and the roof had sagged. Harry had to come too, of course. Frank had been helping Nonno and the others dig out some of the new vines, but most of them were buried so deep that they had drooped by the time they reached them. The leaves looked odd, like they were burnt, not frozen under cold snow for weeks. The stakes were stacked in a pyramid, the wires rolled up, and the vineyard abandoned. Canigou was as it always was. So were me and Frank and Harry. I thought I got the message that the mountain gave me – that things should stay the way they were.

I wasn't lonely at all while I waited for Peter to come back for the summer because there was always Frank and Harry, and even Bruno. I told Frank about Bruno. I don't know why I hadn't already asked him what to do about the old drooly dog barking in the lane on my way to school every day.

"He's a guard dog, it's hard for him to be any other way," Frank said, when I told him about the sherbet lemon and trying to make friends with Bruno. "All that bark might just be for show too. He's probably glad to talk to someone."

"Maybe that's it," I said. "He's on his own so much. I mean, I expect he's lonely and, you know, needs someone who will be like the other half of him."

"You mean Bruno's the cherry and he needs some almonds," Frank said, laughing.

"Exactly. And maybe *I* could be his almonds." I thought for a minute. "How am I going to do that, though?"

"Just like you're doing with Harry," he said, knowing how well Harry and I had been getting on.

Frank said animals don't actually recognise the words we say, but when they feel something about us, it goes straight inside of them and they understand us.

"You're right," I said. "But I think I'll need something sweeter than lemon sherbets to make friends with Bruno."

"Good point," Frank smiled.

I set off to see Bruno with half of my croissant.

"Hello, Bruno, it's me, Hope," I said, standing in the lane quite a long way off, trying not to feel worried about his teeth. "I think you're very handsome and you should be proud of your shaggy fur and maybe, one day, when you don't bark quite so much, I'll bring a brush and make it even smarter. You'd like that, wouldn't you?"

He snatched up the croissant I threw him, wolfed it down, and barked for me to go.

I went back and told Frank.

"Give him time," he said. "Everything and everyone can change. Bruno just hasn't worked you out yet."

"I get the picture," I said. "I haven't worked him out yet either."

"Sure you will though."

I kept it up, every day, giving Bruno half my breakfast. I said nice things to him in between his barks, so we kind of had a conversation, even if I didn't think he was listening to me very well.

"Yes, I know, you're guarding the field," I said. "But I'm not going through the field, Bruno. Honest."

But still, we did start to make some progress, because although he barked, he stayed by the gate and let me go past him up the lane, which meant I didn't have to go through the hedge and take the long way round to school.

I was making progress with Harry, too. There was still one habit that I couldn't help him break though. When I let Harry out of the shed in the morning, he still trotted off to the trailer instead of going straight to the meadow. Carrots and apples didn't mean anything, or at least not as much as a drive up and down the lane.

"One thing at a time," Frank said. "This habit's probably going to be the hardest of them all to change."

With Marianne and Frank either side of me, we watched the mountains from the roof one night in June. The people from the villages all around lit bonfires on the peaks of the Pyrenees, as they did every year on that day, and we cheered when Canigou burned gold on the top. It was like a giant chain of fairy lights being turned on slowly, one at a time, stretching right across the skyline as far as we could see. I thought of how big those mountains were, how strong, how safe I felt right where I was.

I dreamed of me and Marianne, Frank and Harry travelling to the places Frank had told me about, the places where his shoes had once left their prints in the ground. My dreams were as bright as the photographs my mother took of the mountain.

I didn't think about the things I couldn't see off the edge of the shiny paper.

9.

It was summer by now and I was still sleeping up on the roof terrace when one morning I heard Frank talking to Harry down on the drive.

"You gotta choose, Harry," Frank said. "You gotta choose."

When I leaned over the roof tiles this is what I saw: Frank standing with his long legs spread, hands on hips, stopping Harry from getting in his trailer.

I ran downstairs and my mother asked, "What's going on outside?"

"*I'm* supposed to be training Harry," I called back.

Out front, Harry had his head down, swaying side to side, trying to get past Frank.

"Why did *you* let him out today, Frank?" I said. "And why aren't you letting him into the trailer?"

"D'ya think I've fooled him all this time that he's been anywhere else but here?"

"No, but if you drive him around for a bit then he's happy and he'll go down to the meadow by himself like he usually does."

"He's had a heck of a long time to get used to staying."

Which of course he had. Which of course meant something especially to me. To me, Frank wanted

Harry to finally understand that they weren't going anywhere.

People say donkeys are stubborn but, when I watched Frank and Harry holding their ground, I couldn't say which one of them was the most stubborn.

"I thought *I* was supposed to be teaching Harry," I said. "I could do it. I just need some more time to work it out with him."

"I know, Hope, but I figured this habit is down to me and Harry."

There was a part of the world of Frank and Harry that still belonged only to them.

All morning the two of them faced up to each other, although Harry never did look Frank in the eye, each of them determined about their own things. Frank took off his hat, wiping at the sweat, refusing to let Harry pass. The poor donkey swayed, stepping to the side, swaying the other way, trying to get to the trailer. I felt how much Harry wouldn't give up on what he wanted, right through my skin and bones into the middle of me.

Frank was never mean to Harry. Never. He didn't shout, he didn't try to push Harry away or trick him, although by lunchtime Marianne and I tried to persuade Frank to give the donkey treats that we knew he loved, offering to lay a trail of apples to the meadow.

"Harry's gotta work this out himself," Frank said.

Why was this different to Bruno? Why was this different to all the other things I had slowly, bit by bit, trained Harry to do?

"Try again another day, let *me* try again another day," I suggested. "He doesn't look ready yet."

Frank said, "When d'ya think he will be?"

I mean, I got it. It was daft that Harry still thought they were moving on. But I found it harder and harder to watch the battle of wills as the sun got higher, the dust finer, while Harry swayed in the endless heat.

I wanted to stand up for Harry, to say to Frank, *Why do you have to do it? Why, like this?* But it felt like one of those conversations I had with my mother when I'd said, "Why are the vines blue in your painting?" and she'd said, "You have to stop looking at the green to see the blue," and I'd said, "But they *are* green!" and she'd say something else, but all I could hear was *Blah blah blah*, adult things – Marianne things – things that didn't make any sense.

I watched from the roof throughout the day while Frank told Harry over and over, "You have to let it go, Harry. You have to let it go."

I knew Harry could hear Frank, the way he said those words again and again, and I knew that the way Frank said them meant something else I didn't understand. But Harry wouldn't back down.

The sun went down behind Canigou, making blue shadows everywhere. At last Harry stood still for a long time, head hanging down, tired and dirty from all the dust he'd kicked up. Then Harry breathed a big bellyful sigh and turned and headed to the meadow by himself. All I'd done was watch, but I felt exhausted and confused. Not because Frank didn't let me do it, or because of how sad and beaten Harry looked when he changed his mind and slowly walked away from the trailer, but because I felt I would never truly understand what made Frank block Harry's way all day.

I didn't know who to go to first. In the end I

held on to Frank and Frank held on to me and said, "He did it."

And I said, "No, you did it."

Marianne was on the porch holding out a glass of wine for Frank.

"I suppose Harry changed his mind in the end because he was hungry," she said.

But I knew that nobody else could have changed Harry's mind but Frank.

Under a blanket between Marianne and Frank on the porch, I was drifting with sleep, when Frank said, "You'd better take Harry in now, Hope."

Marianne stopped me, which was extremely unlike her.

"After a day like that, don't you think you ought to take him in, Frank? What if Harry's in a temper, or tired and grumpy. He might not be his usual self."

Frank looked troubled by what she said.

"He's himself all right."

"I don't want Hope getting hurt."

Frank looked at my mother as if he was disappointed that she'd ever think Harry would use his hooves or teeth to hurt *anyone*, let alone me, or that Frank would put me in any danger.

"He wouldn't hurt me, would he, Frank? And I want to do it, it's *my* job," I said, throwing off the blanket and rubbing my eyes.

"Frank?" my mother said, in that way that makes you know there are lots of other words hidden.

Frank eventually said, "Hope knows what to do. Harry won't hurt her."

"I'll be fine," I said, "You'll see."

They talked quietly as I walked away. I didn't doubt how safe I was with Harry. Not even the tiniest bit.

Harry looked up as I got closer. He seemed as sweet as always, like he didn't blame me at all. Unspoken, I knew we both had a strong feeling that something important had happened that day. It didn't change anything between me and Harry, but somehow I felt that Harry was bound to me even tighter, that Frank had let a little bit more of Harry go and now that bit belonged to me.

I tapped Harry twice on his left shoulder and he followed me.

My mother had gone inside.

"Harry and me, I think we're cherries and almonds now, Frank. We're more when we're together."

He nodded.

I wished Marianne had stayed to see how good Harry and I were together. She didn't get me, not like Frank did.

Harry went straight to Frank for his goodnight scratch and cuddle. Nothing changed what they had together, even if they'd disagreed all day long. Frank said the magic words, "G'night, Harry," and I led him over to his shed.

"What about tomorrow?" I asked Frank, thinking of Bruno and our slow progress. "Do you think Harry will still go back to the trailer in the morning?"

"He's made his choice," Frank said, so quietly I wasn't sure he'd meant me to hear. "And he'll stick by it."

10.

THE FOLLOWING MORNING FRANK, HARRY AND the trailer were the first things on my mind because I wondered if yesterday's battle had been worth it. Frank had been so sure Harry's old habit had gone, but I wasn't. All the other things I taught Harry to do had taken months; small steps, a little bit at a time.

I ran downstairs in my pyjama shorts and top,

and let Harry out of the shed. Frank was in the doorway of the guesthouse, watching. I think we both needed to know.

Harry glanced at the trailer, his head low as he passed, but he didn't stop. He walked all the way down to the meadow by himself.

To me, seeing him choose not to go to the trailer was as if Harry had won a race, or completed some big achievement, and I knew that he'd never have to go to the trailer again. I cheered, without really knowing exactly why it was so important that Harry was free from his old habit.

"Harry didn't even look back," I called to Frank.

Frank stood there for quite a while staring at Harry as if he was sad that Harry had given up hope of wanting to go for a ride in the trailer again, as if that wasn't what Frank had wanted all along. I couldn't even explain to myself how

Frank just standing there made it seem as if Harry had done something wrong, but it did.

Frank went off with the trailer to sell it. He wasn't going to need to drive a stubborn donkey up and down the lane pretending they were actually going somewhere any more.

Then my mother was calling me from the balcony of her studio, saying, "Peter's coming!" and I ran to meet him.

My best friend arrived home in a stream of dust as his father drove him up the hairpin bends of the mountainside to stay with his grandparents for the summer.

I ran across the meadow, through the hole in the fence and all the way to the other side of the vineyard to meet the car coming around the corner. I shouted to Peter, "We've got the whole of the summer, Peter, every single day to spend together!" and he shouted back through the open window, "I'll be ready in an hour!" Then his father said something over his shoulder, and Peter called again, "Make it two hours."

"Meet me at the waterfall," I said. "I'm bringing Harry. I've got something to show you."

Sometimes two hours is a very long time to wait.

I wanted to show Peter all the things that Harry and I had learned together since he'd been away. To make him part of me and Harry too. I thought he'd love it, having Harry around us even more.

It usually took Peter and me a few days after he'd been away to find the place where we were easy in each other's company, not talking about anything at first other than what we'd been doing since we were last together. But soon the sunshine made us dream and we'd end up making plans for every summer together until we were ninety-nine years old.

The sun climbed and shrank the shadows across the vineyards and the ground was blurred with haze. I called Harry up from the meadow and strapped felt pads over his back so he could carry my bags – towels, drinks, and a change of clothes, nothing heavy.

Marianne watched us from the balcony.

"When are you coming back?"

"I don't know. Later," I said.

"Don't be too long," she said, but I didn't ask why, and Harry and I set off to the waterfall because I couldn't have waited a minute longer.

There was a new tyre on the end of the rope swing. New rope too. Bright blue, tied neatly around and around the branch in a different place, further along from the grooves of the previous swing.

"Look what Frank did, Harry," I said, because only Frank would have done that for us.

There was plenty of grass nearby, trees with some shade for Harry, so I left him to graze while I unpacked the bag, and waited for Peter.

I had no watch but it seemed a long time had gone past before I decided to strip down to bikini top and shorts and take the first plunge into the water, swimming down to the bottom.

The waterfall in summer was hardly a waterfall, but the smooth flat stone about three metres above my head was wide, and a thin spill of water trickled over it. Harry came around the side of the pool, to the shade near where I was, to drink from the clear shallows.

He blinked when I sent a small shower of water to cool his back, but of course didn't look at me. I thought he'd like it, to feel the drops on his dusty fur. I watched him quietly wander back to the grass, his spindly legs holding up the barrel of his belly. Right then, floating on my back in the pool, avoiding the glints of sunlight between the leaves, I thought of another surprise for Peter. Something I felt tall enough to do now.

"What do you think, Harry?"

He looked up, still munching.

"I could do it now, couldn't I?"

Barefoot, I climbed the side of the waterfall, clinging at roots and finger holes in the rocks. At the top the flat rock was slippery green, but I managed to make my way along the shallow spill. It felt good sitting on the edge of the waterfall, high above our place, ready to surprise Peter when he came.

The sun made sharp scorching rays and I was getting bored just sitting there. Peter should have been here by now and I hadn't brought anything else with me to do.

"Where is he?" I said to Harry. "He said he'd be here. Why isn't he here?"

I waited, planning my surprise.

Peter didn't see me at first.

"I'm up here! Where have you been, Peter? You're always late." Which wasn't true, but he had more family commitments than me when he was staying at his grandparents for the summer.

He'd been running. I knew he'd be surprised that I was up on the waterfall but he seemed more shocked than I expected, probably because he wanted to be first.

"Look!" I pointed at Harry. "Harry carried my bag. You wait until you see what else he's learned."

Peter took his time, stroking Harry, talking to him quietly.

"Water's lovely, I already tested," I grinned. "Get in."

Peter hesitated, then dropped his bag and slowly took off his T-shirt, already wearing his long swimming shorts. He stood there for a second looking up at me, and I said, "You're so serious! What are they teaching you at boarding school with all those boring boys? Everything's the same as it always was. Me and the mountain and the vineyards. Have you forgotten us?"

He stood there, staring at the water like he'd never been here before.

"Come on, Peter!"

"I'm coming, I'm coming…"

At last he ran into the water, making as big an

entrance as he could by turning and falling on his back with his arms out.

"Summer has officially started!" he shouted, leaping back up.

"It already started *hours* ago," I said. "You need to catch up!"

"Watch this." He climbed on to a small rock beside the pool and jumped in. Pathetic. Last year he would have run at full pelt, holding his knees to his chest, bombing the surface and sending a tall spout of water nearly up to the top of the waterfall.

"Watch *this*," I said, carefully sliding my feet towards the edge.

"You're not going to jump, are you?"

"I might."

"Wait! Let me check for rocks underneath first."

He swam under the water, was gone for a few

seconds. It was just like Peter to do these things, but also not like this – not with a wobbly voice and in the panicky way he swam to the side.

"There's nothing under there. It's safe," he said.

"I know, I checked earlier."

"You really going to jump?"

"Think I'm scared?"

"You were before."

"I've grown taller," I said, laughing. "I bet I'm taller than you again."

"Wait! No, wait!" he shouted, scrabbling out and climbing up the rocks. "I'm coming too."

"I'm going to jump! I'm going to jump!"

"Please wait, Hope!"

"OK, OK, hurry up then!"

Beside me on the ledge, he held out his hand and I took his.

When I think about it now, I can still remember

how he looked at me, how he held on to me with his brown eyes, as if he wouldn't let me fall without him.

"Ready?" I said, but he didn't answer. "Sometimes, Peter, you just have to jump."

It was me who moved first to jump, but we rose and fell together, sinking with a whoosh and a gurgle into the cool water and the bubbles of air, touching and bouncing off the bottom. We came to the surface, face-to-face and, close-up like that, he didn't look like Peter from a few months ago at all.

"What's wrong, Peter?"

"You have to go home, Hope."

The sun was falling out of the top of its curve but it was still early.

"Why?"

"Before I came here I went to your house to..."

I waited, watched him turn away from what he was about to say. "Well, it doesn't matter why, but I heard them talking. I didn't mean to listen but I heard anyway. Everything isn't the same as it was."

"You're right, it's better, wait until you see what Harry..." I trailed off, looking at his shocked face.

Peter shook his head, as if Canigou had turned to dust.

"I saw Frank with his travelling bag. He's leaving. He's waiting for you and Harry."

11.

WHILE I RAN, I THOUGHT OF ALL THE CRAZY village dogs barking because of the snow that time on the mountain. I saw it in Peter's eyes too. Maybe Bruno had actually been barking *because* he knew the avalanche was coming. Maybe, like me, he'd felt Canigou shift. In the end there was nothing even a mountain could do about keeping Frank, Harry and me together.

Even though Peter wasn't supposed to know before me, I felt weak with being the last to hear. The last to know. The last to see Frank outside the guesthouse, his packed bag at his feet, his passport in his hands.

Half a meadow between us, the distance when Frank saw me too, when I couldn't run any more, when he walked to meet me and to leave me, when what was about to happen couldn't be stopped. I turned away, as if that would change things. I ran again to circle around him because I wanted to get to the house to go up to the roof where all the things were as I expected them to be.

Canigou.

Meadow, vineyards, plane trees, roofs.

Humming bird, the letter H, mermaid, donkey, cherries, knot.

All of the things I fitted together with.

When our paths crossed, and I couldn't avoid what was heading towards me, I couldn't find the words to say what I was feeling inside, wanting to hold on to Frank and hating him for leaving.

"Let me go," he said softly, holding me tighter. "You gotta let me go."

I shook my head and shook my head and the words didn't come out and he didn't apologise for anything and I couldn't let go and what else could I say but, "No. Never."

"Something in me I can't change. I'm sorry, Hope."

I pulled away and punched him but it was nowhere near hard enough to match what had hurt me, and I suddenly felt like he was holding me too tight, so I shouted, "Let *me* go!"

And he said, "I've been trying to," and then

he looked at my hands and I followed his eyes to his shirt, all screwed up in my fists, and I realised it wasn't him holding on any more at all.

The muffled clop of hooves tripping across the gravel reminded me that it wasn't just Frank who was going to leave. All the pairs would be broken, everything undone. How could he have let me get so close to Harry and then take him away too?

"Hope!" Frank called as I ran. "Talk to me!"

"Leave her, Frank," Marianne said.

I ran from them both, up to the studio, because I knew Frank wouldn't follow me there. I wanted to be with him. But I also wanted to be as far away from him as possible. I curled on the sofa but even the cushions wouldn't soften the blow.

Soon, I felt my mother lie down and curl around my back. I slept so I didn't have to feel anything, say anything. I felt her leave and come back again.

"He's gone," she whispered. Her words went into my ear and fell the whole way down my insides like a cold, heavy avalanche.

I slept so it would be dark and I'd forget who I was; that I was Hope Malone, aged twelve, with stupid ideas about mountains and cherries and people who fitted perfectly together. So I would feel less me. Less Hope. Hopeless.

12.

My mother once told me that when she first flew over the snowy Pyrenees mountains she thought they looked like a safe place high up for us to live and that's what made her move us here. We'd be untouchable by anyone else, she'd said. No clocks or hurry, deadlines or commitments, or anything else other people might want her for. Although we were both born in England, my mother and I moved to France when I was eight. Artists do things all of a sudden like that.

I hadn't really fitted in well anywhere, or had many friends, because we had moved quite a lot before that too, so I never got much chance. It was easier to be Hope Malone, alone, than always leaving people behind anyway. Here in France was the longest we'd stayed anywhere.

Most of the girls at my new school didn't take much notice of me at first, as though I was just like one of the tourists on a coach trip to the vineyards and would be leaving again soon. I learned to speak French quickly and after a while they got used to me being there, but they still hardly noticed me. And then I had Frank and Harry and Peter and they were all the friends I wanted.

My mother began to sign her name on her

paintings – Marianne M – with the strokes of the Ms like mountain peaks, as if Canigou had become part of her because she had looked at it for so long. I got that. We felt the same about the mountain.

She said that the houses and the village wedged between the vineyards and the groves of the rocky mountainside protected us. Maybe it was for a completely different reason, but I had felt safe here too, high up, surrounded by things that made sense to me. Me and Canigou. Me and Frank. Me and Harry. Things that made me feel more me.

"Are they coming back?" I asked Marianne, wishing I'd said things to Frank, wishing I'd tried again to find a way to stop him from leaving. Or Canigou had.

She caught my hand. "He'd been saying for a while that he had to leave, but..."

"That day of the avalanche?" I guessed.

She sighed. "We've not really been together since then."

It felt like the air had gone from the room. I went out to the balcony because that's where I knew I could breathe. She had no idea how much what she said hurt me.

"He tried to change but he always was a travelling man."

Marianne's studio was crammed with pictures, postcards, photographs she took, and objects she had collected that she liked or that inspired her, all collected together. On the walls were either art or the materials she used to make art, splattered or spilled, marking every surface. Although Frank had lived here for three years, he'd left the biggest invisible mark.

When I look back now at the three years we'd all spent together, when everything and everyone seemed the same, it was like a painting that my mother had made. Not all the colours made sense, and you couldn't see what else was going on off the edges of the canvas.

"Where have they gone?" I said.

I heard her walk across the floorboards, on to the rug, floorboards again, and felt her close behind me.

"It's just you and me, like it always was."

I didn't know why, but the pair of us, me and my mother, didn't feel right. Like we were tomatoes and cherries.

I could have stayed quiet but then she leaned on me, resting her cheek on my head, gripping the tops of my arms like *she* might fall off the balcony if it wasn't for me standing there.

She said, "Don't worry about me, I'll be all right," and something burst.

"I know *you* will!"

I felt her jerk slightly, as if she realised how stupidly selfish she sounded.

"We never really needed anybody else before Frank and Harry, not really, and we won't again. You've got me and Peter. That's all you need. I always knew it could never last with Frank and I'm surprised he stayed as long as he did."

"You just don't get me at all!" The words began to spill. "Did you ever think... have you ever even once thought that Frank and Harry weren't here just because of you? I mean, Frank stayed because of you, and he had friends and people to drink beer with and lots of jobs..." I couldn't get out what I wanted to say. And it hurt too much to realise, as I thought it, that I had no right to say that Frank stayed because of me too. There wasn't even a word for us.

I remembered that Frank had told me it was Harry who had decided they would stay. But I knew that meant Frank too. Where one was, you were sure to find the other.

Marianne turned me around in her arms.

"I didn't know how much Frank meant to you. I mean, I did, but I thought you'd be used to..." She tailed off as I looked up at her.

"I'm not like you!"

It was my weapon against her and I'd rarely used it. I was nothing like her, especially not that minute. I didn't want to be somebody who was used to leaving people, or people leaving. Not this person and this donkey.

"You can let people go easily. You let them all go and every single time you've told me *you* were happy about it. But I've had nobody for me. Not even you, really."

She looked like a bee had stung her, but I couldn't stop.

"And did you do anything to make Frank *want* to stay?" I wanted her to take the blame because otherwise it meant Frank hadn't wanted to stay for either of us. "I never argued with him, or sulked in my room for days on end, or made life difficult for him."

Either she wasn't listening or I wasn't saying what I was trying to say, because she didn't react.

"Frank *chose* to stay..." but I couldn't continue. It also meant he had chosen to leave *me* as well as her.

There was a silence as I realised what this meant, and while all my breath was breathed out without the rest of the words.

"He didn't leave because of you," she said softly, her hands up as if she might catch me. "He *stayed* because of you and Harry. He said you both needed the same things. To have somewhere safe and solid, to show you there were people you could trust." She sighed. "He didn't think this through, did he? I mean, in the end... perhaps he even made things worse."

I had heard something like that before but couldn't remember when.

"But Frank gets me. He's the only one who really does. I know he does because he asked me to look after Harry, because he let me wear his sheepskin jacket and he never lets anyone borrow it. He talked to me by the fire, about anything, about everything, even when he probably wanted to be alone or with Harry."

I had never doubted the ways in which we had fitted together and it was only now I realised that it didn't matter if there wasn't a word for who

Frank and I were to each other. I had felt it. I was sure he had too.

I still hadn't said what was really on my mind.

"Mum?"

Occasionally I called her Mum. Only to be used in emergencies, and this really was one. She held me, kissed my hair and wrapped her arms like fabric around me.

"Antony and Martin—"

"Marvin," she interrupted, and I recalled him and his noise and curly hair and guitar.

"All of them. I let them go. It was easy. I only ever *liked* them a bit. They were *your* boyfriends, they didn't mean anything to me. And I can't explain, but I did sort of mind them leaving too. Except when Rafael left, I didn't like him at all." The tears fell and it was a kind of relief to get past being angry and feel what I really felt. Hurt.

"Frank and Harry, they were both like other halves of me. The halves that made me feel like all of me."

She looked lost. No words or answers for me.

Instead she led me to the sofa and lay me across her lap and we tried to get comfortable while something inside was almost too painful to bear. I didn't know *how* to be me without Frank and Harry.

13.

IT FELT LIKE THE NIGHT SKY HAD FILLED IN ALL the gaps tightly around me. I needed some air to untangle from the sweat sticking me and my mother together. I went downstairs.

Outside, I saw something that made no sense to me at all.

I ran back towards the studio, calling, "Mum, come outside!"

I half dragged her down the stairs to see what was there at the front of the house.

Harry.

Still with the picnic and my clothes on his back, he was standing near the bench where Frank would have met him before Harry went to bed. Marianne and I froze. Harry raised his head, turned his tall ears forward and stared at the bench. He took a couple of steps, ears twitching, head turning, slowly looking and looking for what he expected to see. But Frank wasn't there, and Harry didn't understand.

Harry took another step, and, feeling nobody rub his neck and forehead, stayed right where he was. He sniffed the ground as if Frank's feet might be there too but he just couldn't see them.

"What's Harry still doing here?" my mother gasped, but I didn't know either.

Not knowing what else to do, I unbuckled the backpack, tapped Harry's shoulder and asked him to follow me to the shed, but Frank missing, with his goodnight affection gone, Harry wouldn't move.

"I don't understand," my mother murmured. "Frank didn't tell me that he was leaving Harry behind."

"He needs to go in the shed though. Please, Harry," I said.

For the first time I suddenly wondered if the reason Harry had gone to the trailer every morning was because he'd never wanted to stay. I had no idea how Frank would have got Harry to stay here after he'd left.

I tapped Harry's shoulder, more firmly this time. He looked at my hand. He didn't understand why his best friend was missing.

"Oh, God, it's the trailer all over again," Marianne said.

"Get some carrots and apples."

She came back with the things I'd asked for, but Harry wouldn't be moved, even by the treats. He just stood there, ears twitching, blinking slowly.

Frank never got angry with Harry and I knew that wouldn't be the right thing to do. But what could I do about a stubborn donkey that got left behind?

"Do what Frank did," Marianne said.

Sitting on the bench I held out my hands but Harry continued to stand as if frozen-still with confusion.

I tried again by copying what Frank had done, crossing my ankle over my knee, arm across the back of the bench, and then leaned forward. Harry let me rub his neck and the fringe between his ears, and I whispered, "Please, Harry, let me say goodnight for Frank."

I tried every single way. With Marianne sitting on the bench and me beside Harry, tapping his shoulder after Marianne had said goodnight. I tried an Australian accent. We tried everything to make the situation most like what Harry was used to.

We weren't strong enough to help him. We weren't *stopping* Harry from doing something, like Frank had when he'd refused to let Harry go to the trailer. We were trying to *make* Harry do something new, and that seemed like a whole other set of rules that none of us understood.

"He'll have to stay out here," Marianne said at last.

"We can't just leave him."

"He'll go back to the meadow." She rubbed her forehead. "He'll be fine. It's not cold. Donkeys live outdoors all the time in the wild."

"He's not a wild animal," I pleaded. "He's never lived in the wild. He's always had people making choices for him."

"He's a donkey, Hope. Put a halter on him and lead him in."

I noticed the frustrated way she had of not being able to sort things out, how she used to be years ago. Frank had made life easier for her too.

She went inside, leaving Harry to me.

I had no other ideas until frustration made up my mind for me too.

I put the harness on his head.

"Come on, Harry, you have to go in," I said. The rope went taut and slipped out of my hands when Harry threw up his head. I looped the rope around my hand a couple of times. With the rope held tight and supported by my shoulder, I turned my back, dug my feet in and leaned away from Harry's weight. Harry raised his head and pulled away from me again, standing his ground.

"Harry, please! Frank would want you to go in too."

I turned to face him. The tightening rope squashed my knuckles together and pinched my skin.

"Goodnight, Harry!"

I pulled. Harry's rear end lowered and he dug in with his hooves.

Teeth gritted, I shouted, "Harry! You have to!"

I yanked the rope hard. Harry threw his head up, wrenching me back so suddenly that I ended up sprawled at his feet in the dirt. Small, with spindly legs, but so strong. Harry took one tiny step away from me. It made me cry into the dust, that he had only moved inches, just enough to take care not to stand on me, but not enough to get any closer to the stable, or away from where Frank was supposed to be.

I gave up. Not on Harry. I gave up being upset with him for being a donkey that found it hard to break old habits. Maybe Harry and I were the most alike of all the pairs.

Instead, I brought the pail of water out of the stable and armfuls of straw. I collected blankets from Frank's old bed, draped one over Harry's back and one around my shoulders. I tucked my knees and nose into the smell of Frank, and prepared to sit out the night with Harry.

14.

"HEY, I CAME TO SEE IF YOU WERE OK. I'M sorry about today, about Frank, I mean," Peter said, and then his eyes opened wide when he saw Harry.

I'd forgotten all about Peter. It must have been hard for him to overhear Frank saying that he was leaving and then carry those words all the way to the waterfall and give them to me.

"What's Harry still doing here?"

Peter knew that Frank and Harry were always together. It didn't make sense at all that Frank hadn't taken Harry with him.

"I don't know, but he won't go in. He won't have a drink and he won't eat and he won't lie down," I said. "I've tried everything."

"Do you think that maybe Harry needs to have a different home altogether?"

I wasn't sure exactly what he meant by that but it made me think. What would I do without Peter?

"You're quite clever, did you know that, Peter Massimo?"

I threw off the blanket.

"Harry needs a new house," I said.

I collected big canvases that Marianne had thrown out, and Peter helped me thump old posts of wood into the ground to lean the canvases against, while the dark made walls around us. We pegged another blanket over the top so Harry was enclosed, so it seemed more like he was inside.

"If you can't get the donkey in the stable," Peter said, "you can build a stable around the donkey." He laughed and it suddenly seemed so funny, the bench forming the back wall of the new stable, with us still sitting on it, peering under the blanket roof with Harry contained inside. Harry was surrounded by half-finished paintings of mountains and vineyards that made him look like a giant donkey among them.

Peter talked to me jokily, the way he always did. Shall we drag the meadow over like a grassy rug? Brick by brick, should we move the guesthouse next to Harry's new house? I laughed, but that made my eyes fill up, because I wasn't really laughing. I was just letting things out and there were so many feelings to come out that it felt like too much for me.

"Peter, stop," I said.

He fed an apple to Harry that Harry lazily took, as if it was any other apple and not the first he'd eaten since Frank had left.

"Why do you think Frank left Harry behind?" Peter asked.

He nudged me but I was numb with something other than cold. I pushed away the things I didn't want to see.

"Can we not talk about it any more because I feel really bad, I mean, worse than I knew I even could."

Peter pulled the blanket across me so he could put it over himself too.

"You've got dust stuck to your face," he said,

touching his own cheek to show me where the tears had dried.

"Thanks," I said, wiping my face with my sleeve.

Peter sighed.

"So are we going to sit out here with Harry every night? All summer? What about after summer and when it's winter?"

Today was enough to think about, but I felt safer knowing that at least Peter would be here.

"I don't want it to be like this, Peter. It all feels broken in bits."

Peter stayed quiet. I buried my face in the blanket, to stop the tears, to not cry in front of him.

"Does Marianne know where Frank has gone? I mean, in case you needed to contact him about Harry, or anything else."

"She didn't say."

I assumed Frank was travelling again. But he hadn't talked of places where he wanted to go, only of those that he'd already been to. I didn't think Frank had anywhere left to travel. I also realised I had no idea how big the world was.

"What about tomorrow?" Peter said. I knew he needed to know what all this would mean about us and our summer plans.

"I don't know. I had it all planned, but not planned. Just me and you and none of this."

It felt strange to think of somebody gone. It wasn't a hole that Frank had left. Inside I felt crammed full of things I didn't want to feel, and I felt if I started to let them out I'd be buried underneath it all.

In lots of ways, Frank had also been family without it ever having been like the law, or your genes, or whatever it is that makes a family belong to each other. It's what it had felt like to me, because every day was really no different to when Peter went home to his grandparents after a day of adventure with me. Except his family had proper names for who they were.

"I was going to show you what I've taught Harry to do. I've been working hard every day, looking after him."

I told him all the things I'd had to do to get Harry to trust me. Peter thought for a minute.

"Do you think Frank left Harry on purpose?" he asked.

"Why would he do that?"

"For you, Hope."

I shook my head.

"Why else did he ask you to train him and look after him?"

All the time, had Frank been trying to find a

way to make Harry get closer and closer to me? So Harry would let him go?

I couldn't accept that at all. How could he do that to Harry?

Harry's head still hung, but his ears twitched at every tiny sound in the distance, like he was expecting to hear Frank's jeep rumble up the drive.

I couldn't explain it, but that felt like the most hurtful thing, for Frank to have left Harry behind.

I threw off the blanket, startling Harry who twitched his ears back.

"Harry should be with Frank. Frank should be with Harry."

These were the words I said out loud. But there was much more I couldn't say, couldn't hope for, and couldn't choose.

I nearly knocked the bench over scrabbling to get out of Harry's temporary stable.

"Sorry, Harry."

"Hope, wait a minute." Peter had climbed out over the back of the bench and was now standing in front of me. "Where exactly are you going?"

"To find Frank."

"But how?"

I wasn't annoyed by Peter trumping me with more sensible answers than I had. I was more annoyed with myself for not thinking of this earlier, for knowing that I'd wasted time while miles and miles had stretched out between me and Frank, Frank and Harry.

"We can make a proper plan in the morning," Peter said as if he had the final decision. "I'll ask Nonno, I'm sure he'll drive us to look for Frank."

Peter looked all around the drive. The trailer was gone. It had been gone for months. But I didn't want him to be right about why that was.

"How are we going to take Harry with us?" Peter said.

"We'll find Frank first," I said, agreeing with him in words. "Meet me here in the morning. Ten o'clock. And don't be late."

But I had no intention of waiting for Peter.

15.

ALL NIGHT I STAYED ON THE BENCH BESIDE Harry, trying to figure out how to find Frank, hardly sleeping at all. Marianne came out to see if I was OK, but I didn't tell her my plan. She didn't know what to say to me anyway, except to ask if I was warm enough.

I asked her if Frank had said where he was going, but her reply – "Travelling, I didn't ask where,"– disappointed me more than she would ever know.

"Didn't you want to know?" I asked.

"You don't understand," Marianne sighed. "It didn't matter to him where, he just can't help moving on. We're not together any more, Hope, which means he didn't have to tell me."

"Didn't he say *anything*, like he was going back to Australia?"

"He's more likely to have told you than me," she said quietly.

I hated that he didn't have to tell me either.

I decided that somebody in the village must have information and the first part of my plan would be to find out who.

Early the next morning, as soon as the sun peeked over the mountain, I went to the guesthouse and checked everything, looking for any tiny trace that

Frank might have left. Nothing. No clues to where he might have headed. All his old papers burned. The only thing I could think was that wherever he was going, he'd need money to get there.

I took down the canvas board acting as the wall of Harry's stable and led him to the meadow. He was as sweet and gentle as ever again.

"You'd better eat plenty, Harry. You're going to need it. You're going travelling again. I'll be back soon."

His ears twitched. Did he know what I meant?

I ran up to the village. The bank hadn't opened yet. I held my hand over my eyes and peered in the window. Somebody was inside so I knocked hard until he came to the narrow window at the side.

"It's urgent," I shouted. "I need some help."

Monsieur Albert, the bank manager, came out into the foyer.

"Please, Monsieur Albert. It's really important. Open up!"

The door clunked and clicked as it was unlocked and Monsieur Albert poked his head out.

"What's so important at this hour?"

"I wouldn't ask and I know you probably can't tell me because of security or whatever, but it's a matter of… of international importance that I find Frank."

"Frank? Ah, you mean Monsieur Abernathy?"

"Did he come and see you recently?"

"I personally closed the account and told him how truly sorry I was that he felt the need to withdraw *all* of his money at once but, as you know, Frank is a man of few words."

I let how final that sounded sink in.

"Did he say where he was going?" I said.

"It's not my business to pry."

"Did he say *anything*? Anything that might give

a clue as to where he's gone? You see I *have* to find him. He left something behind, something extremely important."

Monsieur Albert folded his arms. "But I don't know, not exactly."

"You do know *something* though? We can't let Frank go without… without this thing." I was unwilling to say it was Harry, guessing that the bank manager wouldn't understand. "Please, it really is the most important thing to Frank ever."

Monsieur Albert unfolded his arms and straightened his jacket.

"I happened to see that after he left the bank… just coming outside for some fresh air, you understand?"

"Yes, what did you happen to see?"

He twiddled his thumbs. "He went to Soleil Travel."

"Thank you!" I was already running down the street.

Frank had taken all his money. He could have gone anywhere in the world, twice around it probably.

Another locked door, but I found a space between the holiday posters and notices to peer in the travel agents, knocking on the window until a lady came out from the back with a cup of coffee in her hand.

She spoke through the glass door after looking at her watch.

"We're not open for another ten minutes."

"I need to talk to you about Frank. It's urgent."

She unbolted the door and came outside.

"You know Frank? Frank the carpenter? He did some work for you."

"I'd hoped he would come and fix the shelves at

home for me too. I'll have to ask Monsieur Dubois now, but he's not as young as he used to be."

"So you know he's gone?"

"Monsieur Dubois?"

"Frank!"

"Oh, yes. He bought a ticket two days ago. Is he really going this time? He cancelled his flight earlier this year at the last minute."

"After the avalanche," I said, the words tumbling out of my mouth as if I couldn't stop them. Had it really only been the avalanche that stopped him going?

"When is his flight?"

She looked at her watch again. "Two o'clock this afternoon."

"Which airport?"

16.

THE AIRPORT WAS ALMOST TWENTY MINUTES' drive away. Too far to walk. Even though Peter had said he was going to ask his grandfather to drive us, it was much more important that I take Harry. Frank surely didn't mean to leave him behind.

The Vilaros' tractor was parked in the gateway of the vineyard. Peter and I had learned to drive it years ago. If Peter was with me, he wouldn't have let me take the tractor, so it was good I'd gone without him. Nothing, nobody, was going to stop me putting Harry and Frank back together. It was the only thing that made sense now.

I drove the tractor up to the meadow, not too close to the house in case Marianne heard, although I didn't actually think she would try to stop me. I collected a few things, and when I came back outside Marianne was stood on the studio balcony.

It had always been Marianne's idea that I should do what I want. I had loads of freedom and she never understood why I didn't use it. Well, I would use it now.

"What are you doing with the tractor?"

"I'm… being creative," I said, not knowing what else to say.

I ran down to the meadow. I knew what I had to do with Harry. I saddled him up with his felt pads, buckled his leather belt, and tied on a small bale of hay and his plastic pail.

"I can't walk beside you because it's too far for me," I said. "So you're going to have to trot to keep up. It's a long way, but I know how strong you are and that you can do it." Harry didn't look me in the eye as I stroked his nose and kissed him. I'd spent so much time with Harry, training him and getting him to trust me, and I felt I knew what was inside that barrel belly, inside his skin and bones. The other half of us. Frank. "When Frank sees you, he'll remember who should be together."

"Hope!" my mother called, running towards us. "Where are you going?"

"Travelling."

"What do you mean, travelling?"

I tapped Harry's shoulder twice, climbed up on the tractor, put the water bottle beside the seat and turned on the engine.

"There's something Harry and I have to do."

"At least take Peter with you," Marianne said. I guessed she knew what I was doing, but she didn't say.

"We can't wait for him. We don't have time."

"What shall I tell him?"

"Tell him… tell him Harry needs a new home. He'll understand."

Harry and I set off down the track, the tractor rattling and spitting up dust, Harry trotting quickly behind me.

17.

We'd gone five kilometres (which I knew because of the sign pointing back up the hill) and were at the junction where you either went further down the mountain or off down a side track towards another vineyard on the lower slopes. I looked over my shoulder for about the hundredth time to see Harry behind me, head down as always, patiently trotting behind or waiting for the tractor to move on. I felt he knew exactly where we were going.

The heat was wriggling off the tarmac as the sun climbed and baked the olive trees and soil. It smelled like one great big kitchen, like one great big pie, full of flavour.

We turned down the mountain. The road was steep and windy, a little wider, but not much. Not many cars came up here, usually only people who lived in the villages or worked in the vineyards. I looked back and Harry was still trotting behind, bits of not-so-tightly bound hay flapping at the sides of the small bale on his back. As we went around a hairpin bend, we met a coach coming towards us. I slammed my foot down to stop. We couldn't pass.

People were peering out of the tinted windows. The driver threw his hands up, flicking his wrists towards me to tell me to reverse back up. But I couldn't get the gearstick into reverse. I got off the tractor and asked Harry to follow me back to a narrow verge, where I left him in the shade. I went back to the tractor and got some water and put it into his pail.

The driver got out of the cab.

"Are you going to move?" he said.

"Just give me a minute." Truth was, I wanted to give Harry a break, but I was also stalling because I didn't think I'd be able to reverse uphill.

"I have a schedule," the driver said, tapping his watch.

"So do I, but the donkey needs to rest a minute."

Some people got off the coach, muttering in English. A mother and her child went over to pat Harry. Harry looked over to me, as if he was asking, *Will they be kind to me?*

"All right, Harry," I said. "They won't hurt you."

The mother moved the pail of water nearer to Harry but he didn't drink.

I got back up on the tractor. It was much hotter down the mountainside than further up, and already the heat was beginning to sting my face and shoulders and rattle me. And no matter how hard I crunched the gears, all I got was a loud revving from the engine and a grinding sound from the gearbox.

"Should you be driving?" the driver said. "What are you doing driving a tractor down here? Is it allowed on this road?" Several people were talking about whether the tractor was illegally on the road and whether a girl should be driving.

Then I heard someone say, "It's cruel, making a donkey work like that."

The words settled in my stomach and added to the frustration of not being able to reverse the tractor. Sweat ran down my hairline and my neck.

"Look at the creature's heavy load," a woman said. "Poor donkey."

Frank had always told me that pity was the last thing Harry needed. However sorry Frank had felt for Harry, he never once let his donkey give in to what had happened to him in India.

"He needs something to carry," Frank told me once.

I remembered the time a few weeks after they'd arrived, when I'd gone to fetch Frank from where he was working to come down to the meadow because Harry wouldn't stop braying. He was stopped still, his neck and back sagging between his cries, as if he still carried his heavy bricks.

That noise wasn't something I could ignore.

"What's wrong with him, Frank?" I'd said. "Is he hurt? Why is he crying? What's wrong? We need to help him."

"We will."

Frank didn't say anything else. He'd leaned against a fence post, watching. Only once did Harry turn towards Frank, almost looking him in the eye that one time. Harry turned his back, his voice getting hoarser and coarser as time went on.

"He needs something else to carry," was all Frank said in the end.

Harry was given the job of carrying Frank's tools when he had carpentry work in the village, or helping out around the place. Harry never cried again.

* * *

At the side of the road, a group of the passengers gathered around Harry. It was a tour bus, the sign on the front window advertising a trip to the vineyard. They were English tourists, wearing too many clothes and smelling of sun cream and sweet drinks.

"Have we got any apples in the picnic basket?" a pale, round man, with sweat patches on the armpits of his T-shirt, said to his wife and son. "Poor thing. What's there to eat around here? Look. Hardly anything. Give him a sandwich."

I didn't say anything. Not just because Harry and I really had no time for this, but also because I realised that all these people now reaching out and patting Harry had just arrived on this mountainside and in this country, for a week of sunshine and sightseeing, and they only knew a little bit of the story of Harry. They didn't know him like I did. They just looked at the load on his back and a girl making him carry it down the steep mountain road, and decided it was wrong. They couldn't see that Harry needed to do something useful. To stop him feeling sorry for himself.

"The *poor* donkey bites," I lied, because I wanted the tourists to move away from Harry and take their sympathy with them. The son of the sweaty round man pulled his hand and the sandwich away quickly.

"And he kicks," I said, and soon the passengers were re-boarding the coach, muttering things that didn't matter to me and Harry.

I yanked the gearstick until it finally crunched into reverse.

The tractor groaned as the tread of the tyres dug in, and I backed it into the layby.

The driver wiped away the sweat on his forehead as the coach inched past, almost touching the rusty arches of the back tractor wheels.

It was the first time I knew for sure that the mountain was my home. Harry and I were about to leave the place where we'd been safe and cared for. The place we knew and fitted with. The first half of the story that we'd gotten used to.

The second half of the story: well, I had no idea how it was going to end, because already deep down I knew I couldn't put things back together how I wanted. Not how I *really* wanted it to end, like it had begun, with all of us coming together.

18.

At the bottom of the mountain road, the junction split north or south for the airport. Fast traffic whizzed by on the main road and blew dust showers over us, the wind catching bits of the hay on Harry's back and pulling them loose.

We were leaving the mountainside. Meadow, vineyards, plane trees, roofs. Canigou.

I looked back, at the landscape, people and animals that I knew fitted around me.

Marianne once took me to a gallery in London to see her paintings. Under the high ceilings she had ten huge canvasses, each a different view of the mountain, painted in Marianne's own way. I'd never seen her paintings like that before, without the jumble of things around them in her studio that had the marks of her paint on everything, so that you could hardly tell what was a painting and what was just paint.

Staring up, it had been like sitting too close to a cinema screen when everything seems to be rushing past too quickly to see exactly what's happening. I think that's what she wanted people to feel. You could see how she'd brushed, like she was furious with the way the things that covered the mountain changed so quickly. But you could also see that the mountain was still there behind the wild brush strokes of reds and yellows and blues, colours that she told me were there but I couldn't see. Behind all the colours, the background to it all, between the thin strokes of the brushes, was the safe, dark rock of Canigou.

I remember thinking *I live there*.

With Canigou behind me, the rest of the world spread out along the busy road leading to cities and the airport. It all looked much bigger than I remembered. It was like standing on the top of the waterfall and not feeling tall enough to jump. Not without Peter. I wasn't sure I could have jumped if he hadn't been there.

I couldn't see how we could travel on that main

road. Not a girl, a tractor and a donkey. Not us by ourselves.

"Harry?" His ears turned forward. "I don't know if I can do it."

I climbed down and sat on the running board and held out my hands. Harry came over and leaned on me.

"I don't know if I'm big enough yet, Harry." He must have heard what was in my voice. He nuzzled in closer, as if he was trying to make us into one strong thing.

Sometimes you've been so busy just trying to make things stay the same that you don't notice you've actually gone and stolen someone's tractor and made a donkey follow you and not thought it would be more sensible to bring someone else with you to help. And that you will have to go back home all by yourself.

"What will I do without you too, Harry?"

I knew Harry was old. Frank said you could tell by his worn, wonky brown teeth. Sitting there with his head on my lap it felt like he was only a little child that I had to take back to where he belonged. We were the same. Feeling small and unprotected without the person who came along and rescued us, and made everything feel safe.

"Hope!"

I didn't know who I expected to see calling my name, but I should have guessed Peter would have come after me. I wasn't really thinking right at all without Frank there.

Nonno pulled up his car beside us and Peter jumped out.

"Didn't think I'd let you go without me, did you?"

I shook my head, not because the answer was

no. Sometimes I was just amazed what he'd do for me.

He sat down, shuffling me up to make room.

"We found you because Monsieur Vilaro came over to say somebody stole his tractor. I guessed it was you and you'd come this way. But Nonno made it all right with Monsieur Vilaro, and you're not in trouble, and somebody will come down to take the tractor back."

"There isn't any other way off the mountain, Peter."

I leaned on him as he scratched Harry's forehead.

"Nonno will take us wherever you want to go, Hope." Peter and Nonno were two special flavours together too.

I couldn't have done it on my own, but there would be no point if I couldn't take Harry.

"It's Harry who has to be with Frank. Look at him. He's the saddest and smallest he's ever seemed. We have to put Harry and Frank back together."

"Where exactly are we going?"

I pointed, the same direction as the sign on the main road.

"The airport."

Peter went back to the car and spoke to Nonno. Nonno flapped his arms and shook his head and talked to Peter in Italian, until he called across, "Is OK, Hope. Bring donkey."

"We'll follow the car. Me, you and Harry. Nonno knows a shortcut off the main road," Peter said, so pleased that he was part of this, and I couldn't think of any reason at all why I'd tried to leave him out.

19.

WE LEFT THE TRACTOR BEHIND.

Harry followed Peter and me into the scrubby patch of ground, cutting across fields and open areas, while Nonno stayed in the car and crawled along the quieter road nearby. Peter talked to distract us from the dust and the heat and the journey ahead.

"What shall we do for our birthdays this year?" Peter said.

Our birthdays were only five days apart, at the end of July.

I knew what was coming next. We had the same conversation every year. I said, "Oh, I don't know," because I knew he already had an answer.

"Nanu asked if you wanted to have your birthday at our house with me."

Having birthdays as close together as ours meant I was used to the Massimos being a kind of ready-made family when it came to having people celebrate around me. My mother wasn't very good at organising things and was quite happy to let the wealthy Massimos make something of the day. Peter's day, anyway, shared by me.

"Can we say it's Harry's birthday as well?" I asked, thinking that after today I would never see him again. "That way we'll always remember him."

Peter loved Harry and he probably would have liked to say he loved Harry as much as I did, but I knew he couldn't have told his family that. His family, and some of the village people who worked on the land, didn't think the same way about donkeys or dogs or any other animals the same way Frank and I did.

The village was like a place from another time long ago, which was why Marianne liked it. It was a place you could stop when you had nowhere else to go. Where you could be an artist, be all of yourself, not have to keep up with things that changed.

The air felt heavy and I wasn't used to being out in the open like that, the heat fizzing and blurring the distance ahead of us. The mountainside was cooler, the view clearer. My legs seemed to be walking by themselves, my feet going forward, pulling me along with them, until the thought that Frank had left Harry behind on purpose made it too hard.

"Peter, I need to stop a minute."

I sank down in the shade of some rocks.

Harry stood in the blazing heat and I got up again to tap his rump gently, so he could choose the shade, pulling some of the hay from his bale and scattering it at his feet.

"I left the water on the tractor."

I sank down beside Harry promising him we would find somewhere to drink, although I knew he could go for hours without water, but Peter ran off towards the car and opened the boot. He'd thought of everything.

Sweat trickled down my face.

"I've told you about Harry, how Frank rescued him from India," I said. "Think about how far they had to come, I mean, thousands and thousands of miles, all the countries they went through to get here. It's like a miracle or something, or like the world knows who makes good pairs, and it doesn't matter how far apart they are, it finds a way to put them together."

"I told Nonno about where they'd travelled from. He said they were lucky to get here at all."

"So why did Frank do all that and then just leave Harry? You don't just leave valuable things behind."

I imagined them, just like we were now, having come much further than we had today. I wondered exactly how much Harry had cost. I rested my face against his, felt the grind of his teeth and jaw as he chewed.

People paid lots of money for Marianne's paintings. It didn't make sense to me, what the same amount of money meant to different people.

"Frank would have given all his money for Harry. He did, didn't he, Harry? Even if that was all he had. You wouldn't understand, Peter."

Peter looked sort of sorry for not understanding. I mean, how could he understand when he had so much?

I wanted this journey to be over. I wanted to go home and find everything as it had been yesterday.

We walked on, Peter a little way behind, his head hanging as low as Harry's. I didn't realise how bad Peter would feel about what I said, and it made me feel bad to think I didn't understand everything about him.

Harry's bale had loosened and was no longer holding together. Wisps left a trail behind us and at first I tried to gather the pieces up, but the hay prickled my arms and stuck to the sweat, and I soon let it drop and ignored what we were losing.

20.

HARRY SUDDENLY STARTED TO BRAY. BEHIND US, he'd stopped.

"Harry, what's wrong?" I said, running back.

"Why's he doing that?" Peter clamped his hands over his ears. "Does he need some more water?" He grabbed the bucket and tipped up the bottle he'd been holding all this time. Harry didn't drink.

"It isn't water he wants, Peter."

At first I thought something had scared Harry, but it didn't take me long to realise that it was nothing like that at all.

"He only did this once before. Frank said he needed a job to do. That's why he used to carry Frank's tools."

I had to speak in the quiet moments between the noisy braying. I didn't have a bag of tools and I wasn't going to give Harry rocks to carry. That would have been wrong, not only because it was pointless (I was sure Harry would have known), but I also didn't want to remind him of the bricks he'd had to carry. Harry had lost his hay, but it wasn't that. It wasn't the same sound as before.

I let him bray for a while, and watched him carefully, like Frank had done before.

"What are you doing?" Peter said.

"I'm listening."

"Are you going deaf? Can't you hear him?"

"I'm listening for something else."

"Like what?"

I listened with my skin and my bones, like Frank told me to. To hear what words weren't coming out into the world, to let Harry's call go right into my ears and all the way inside, to see if I could make sense of it.

"Bruno!"

"Where?" Peter yelled over the din, spinning around and looking. "What do you mean? Bruno isn't here."

"No! Remember Bruno and the avalanche. I don't think he was talking to the mountain at all. He was talking to us, saying to stay with him so he could guard us, because that's what he does best."

Harry brayed, but in between kept turning

towards me and then looking towards the distance.

"Is there another avalanche?" Peter threw his hands up just like Nonno. "Sometimes, Hope Malone, you make no sense at all."

"Not an avalanche."

Peter shaded his eyes as I pointed to the looming shape of an aeroplane above us, heading for the edgeless sky.

"Harry didn't know we were coming to the airport. I mean, he's a donkey, he doesn't know what an airport is."

"No, he doesn't. But all the same…"

What was it about Harry? What was it that made him the way he was? The noise meant something; I just couldn't work out what. Even so, something changed inside. All I could think was that I had no choice but to keep going. There would be a second half to the story, but what?

I couldn't say what I was feeling when Harry turned and looked me in the eye. Maybe he'd never done that before because he didn't need to, because before he'd been happy to go along with what he'd been asked to do. It seemed he wanted me to know something really important, but I couldn't say out loud what I thought he was trying to tell me, because it couldn't be true. Did he really not want to leave?

Up ahead in the distance, I saw Nonno had got out of his car and was waving to us from where he'd parked, pointing to the glass tunnel and stairs that went over the top of the road and into the airport.

"Harry." I knelt down and held his face. He stopped braying. "It's OK. It'll all be OK, I'll be with you."

"Hope?" Peter looked left out. I didn't want that either.

"OK, we're coming. Help me get Harry in the airport."

I tapped Harry's shoulder again. He looked at me and I told him without saying it, that he had to come with me. This time he followed.

I walked beside Harry, my arm over his neck, which Harry knew meant he had to stay right beside me, and we climbed the stairs with Peter going ahead, calling out, "It's OK, Harry. It's safe."

Some people with suitcases were coming in the opposite direction. Peter said sorry to them all and made like a traffic policeman, waving us through and getting everyone to flatten themselves against the sides because we were not about to stop for anyone.

"Stand back," Peter said. "Donkey coming through."

Harry seemed not to notice all the people and the noise, and for a minute I didn't even notice them. It was just me and Harry. On a journey together.

And then I felt panicked, and that feeling got bigger and bigger the closer we got to the airport's glass entrance doors. We could see Nonno, his arms up as if he was cheering us on.

"What do you want to do now?" Peter said.

Just inside the door I could see screens spelling out destinations. Where was Frank going? It was a small airport but I realised it was going to be much harder to find him than I thought.

Peter nudged me. Two security men in uniforms were walking quickly towards us, looking at Harry, one of them speaking into a radio.

I held Harry's ear and wished with everything I had that he would understand what I was trying to say, what I thought he was still waiting to hear.

"G'night, Harry." He hesitated. "G'night!" I smacked him gently on the bum, and he trotted away through the busy airport, ears pricked, skinny tail flicking.

Crowds scattered quickly and a wide path opened up between Harry and the departure gate as he trotted through, as if he knew where he was going. I loved Harry right then more than ever, because he had the same sense of order I did.

I couldn't see Peter. The two security people rushed towards me. And Harry, he just kept going. Another security guard threw himself at the donkey, and Harry dodged to the side and the man slipped over on the floor.

"Find Frank," I whispered as if I had a telephone connection direct to Harry's ears. "Find him, Harry!" For me, too.

The fallen guard got up and he and two more people ran after Harry. A lady guard and one other stayed with me, asking me to come with them.

"G'night Harry!" I shouted, in the hope that Harry knew what he was doing and not just running away from the people panicking around him.

The alarm sounded as Harry's harness buckles set off the metal detector, but Harry didn't stop.

I was led towards the information desk. Peter was already there speaking to the lady behind the desk, and I couldn't hear a word the security people were saying to me because I was too busy watching for Harry, but my ears picked up the message on the speakers:

"*Passenger announcement. Would Frank Abernathy please come to the information desk, or make himself known to airport staff. Frank Abernathy, please make yourself known to any member of staff."*

Through the glass walls of the corridor leading to the departure lounges I saw Harry, still trotting fast, his little spindly legs flicking backwards and forwards as he picked up speed. I'd never seen him run so fast. I didn't even know he could.

Security guards were chasing him, arms out, trying to steer his course. But Harry ducked and swayed and they couldn't hold on to him.

"Go, Harry!" Peter shouted from right by my side.

I recognised his sheepskin jacket first, then his hat, his travelling bag, his long slow stride. Frank was coming along the glass corridor straight towards Harry.

I wriggled free of the lady and ran because I couldn't help myself wanting to be part of Frank and Harry. I followed the path Harry had left between the passengers that had stopped to turn towards the running donkey.

I wanted to throw myself at Frank but I couldn't. At the end of a long journey when you've just kept travelling because you have to, all you really want to do is stop. Maybe that's why Frank had stayed with us. So he could stop and let Harry know they were both where they should be.

"Harry and Hope," Frank said softly as he dropped his bag and met us.

He spoke to the security men who had now surrounded us and asked them to give us a moment.

"You can't go," I said at last. "Not without Harry."

Frank crouched, patted Harry's neck, slowly ran his hand down his smooth grey nose.

"I'm sorry, we should have talked… I should have told you that Harry wants to stay with you."

"But he came here to be with you."

"Because you asked him to."

A moment passed. I hadn't thought of that.

"But he doesn't understand. I can't make him go in his shed without you there to say goodnight to him. He won't go."

Frank smiled a sigh; a brightness was in his eyes.

"Don't you know yet that he won't ever let *you* go?"

"Me?"

The security guards were impatient to have us move, but Frank spoke firmly to them and then told me that we didn't have much time.

"Where are you going?" I asked.

"Travelling."

"What for? Why?"

"There's something in me. I can't change that."

"Everything and everyone can change. You told me that."

He looked away, frowned, but he had no answer. This one thing he'd been so sure of. How come everything could change except him?

"In the beginning, I stayed for Harry. But then… well, you made the world seem simple for me, and I liked that too. But the world according to Hope Malone has grown big enough for both of you now."

He held my hands, looked at them, then at Harry.

"I looked all over the world, all the way from India to France, for someone for Harry, and I couldn't find anyone else I'd trust to leave him with." His voice was quiet until now. Firmly he said, "Harry didn't give up hope..." He turned away from what he was about to say. "He didn't need to. You were with us all that time. One day, I hope that will make sense in your world too."

I held on to Frank, knowing this time that nothing would change his mind. Somehow the hurt soothed, just a little, as I chose to let him go.

"I'll still love you, wherever you are."

I let the words out into the world that I hadn't been able to say before. To let him know how much he meant, whoever he was to me and me to him, because deep down I knew I couldn't choose for him what he did, no matter what. I was just his girlfriend's – ex-girlfriend's – daughter. There isn't a word for who I was to him because it's not a real thing. Just something I made, we made, in our world.

"Won't you miss anyone?" I whispered.

He wiped my tears with a big rough thumb.

"My girl and my donkey," he said. *My girl.*

"Write to me," I said.

"You know I'm not much for writing."

"A postcard, anything. You don't have to write many words, just send some so I know where you are."

He smiled, checked the clock up high on the wall and walked backwards away from us.

"There'll always be a part of me left here."

"But will I see you again?" I whispered.

"G'night, Harry," he said, before turning into the corridor and leaving me and Harry for good.

21.

Peter, Harry and I sat down in the shade of a tree outside the airport. I wondered if Harry had any idea what had just happened as I watched the plane flying Frank away. I told Harry again, "G'night, Harry. Frank said g'night."

I thought if I kept saying it he'd understand it meant goodbye. Or I would. I wasn't sure how much more there was to know about Harry, not after what

Frank told me. Had Harry found Frank at the airport for himself? Or had he found him for me?

Nonno was patiently waiting outside the airport in his car to see what we would do. There was still the journey home to make, a journey I hadn't even thought about for Harry, and now he had the added weight, of being without Frank, to carry home. Right then, Harry seemed really young. I was only twelve but I had to look after him by myself now. That meant I also had to make choices for him too. Maybe that's what Frank had been trying to teach me all along. That even if I live in my own world of stupid questions and ideas, it doesn't mean I'm not strong enough for Harry to rely on me too.

I looked at Peter, who was staring straight ahead at Nonno's car. "Even if you say I was wrong about coming, I'm not going to care," I told him.

"I wasn't going to say that."

"It's what you were thinking."

"It wasn't."

"What are you thinking, then?

"Actually, that you're brave." He turned to face me. "Coming to find Frank, that was harder than just staying at home and being upset."

I liked that he said that and it reminded me that I still had my best friend here with me.

"Peter, will you do me a favour?"

"Of course."

"Go home with Nonno."

"What?" Peter jumped up. "What about you and Harry?"

"I have to make a choice for Harry now. He has to understand that I'm going to look after him, just like Frank would have. And I want to do this by myself."

"Nonno isn't going to let you do that."

"Then explain to him, Peter. Tell him why it's so important to me."

"Explain to me first."

I'd hoped he would understand. I closed my eyes, trying to find the right words.

"Remember that day of the avalanche and Bruno barked at us, and in the end you had to hold my hand and drag me away? Well it's kind of like that. And I don't mean that you should drag me away. I mean, I have to show Harry that I will keep him safe if he comes with me. I think Harry was making all that noise because he did want to stay with me, he just didn't know if I wanted him to stay too. It just feels right, that I take him home by myself."

Peter muttered to himself in Italian so I didn't understand, then walked over to speak to Nonno.

I knew what I had to do. Harry and I could both change, even if Frank couldn't. We had each other and together we had to break our biggest habit of all. Relying on Frank.

I didn't think I'd ever looked past today. When you're ten and eleven and twelve you don't have to. Then it all seems to spread out in front of you, suddenly, all the things that are possible.

Peter came back over. "Hope, Nonno said if you walk home it's going to be harder; you'll be going uphill, it'll take forever."

"It's all been hard, Peter. You can follow me or wait for me by the side of the road, but I have to do it."

"What about Harry?"

Which was exactly what I was thinking. Harry already looked tired. And my shoulders were blistered, the skin on my cheekbones sore, and I ached with the emptiness of Frank being gone.

"I am thinking of Harry, Peter. And we *will* make it. Together."

22.

OUR SHADOWS STRETCHED OUT IN FRONT OF US, long and thin, which meant I didn't have to turn back to see if Harry was still coming, because his shadow walked beside me. Poor Harry. I knew he would feel through his skin and bones, down his ears into every part of him, if I wasn't strong. And it made me stronger. I wasn't going to be afraid. Not with Harry next to me and Peter nearby. Harry had to know he was safe and that I wouldn't let him down.

I saw Peter and Nonno in the car in the distance, slowly moving to the next layby where they could stop but still keep an eye on us.

The spots where we had stopped on the way – for shade by the rocks, the road that we had crossed, where I saw that someone had collected the tractor – felt like major milestones on our trek home.

Halfway up the hill, where we'd met the coach, I went over to the car and asked Peter and Nonno to drive on.

"Please, tell Nonno. We're nearly there."

Something else was on my mind. Somehow it seemed important that my mother saw Harry and me coming home together like this.

Eventually Nonno agreed.

"See you there," Peter said. "I know you can do it."

My legs didn't feel as if they were mine. Like a machine, they just kept going as if they had no choice, or maybe my legs had made the choice and my head hadn't caught up yet. I walked backwards up the mountainside when my calves ached. Harry hung his head low, digging in. I steered him towards patches of grass but he wouldn't eat, and I worried that he felt what I did – that nothing could fill the big hole that Frank had left inside us and that things just wouldn't ever feel like enough again. It's the hardest thing to describe. To want to go home, but to dread being back.

The sun suddenly dipped behind Canigou and all the shadows joined into one. At the same time, I heard a soft sound behind me, like a bag of Nanu's flour being dropped on the floor. Harry had collapsed at the side of the road.

He rolled to his side and laid his head down.

"Harry!" I gasped, running back to him. "Don't give up. You can make it."

Did he feel like I had yesterday, that if he shut his eyes and went to sleep then he could forget that he was a poor grey donkey who had been left behind? I got down beside him, stroked his face. His breathing was shallow; his half-closed eyes blinked slowly.

I'd made him go too far; I'd made him do too much. I looked around for water. I picked some grass, but he closed his eyes and moved his mouth away.

"Please, Harry. It's not far now."

I held the halter and half-heartedly pulled at him. I should have asked Nonno to go and collect a trailer for him, and thinking that made all the strength seep out of me. I let Harry lie back down.

"I'm sorry, Harry. I know it's hard and I didn't mean to hurt you."

He sighed. His eyes flickered and closed again, and I lay down on the side of the road beside him. I had nothing left in my body, not for him or for me.

"We'll just rest, Harry. We'll stay here as long as you need to. It'll be all right."

Gently, I stroked his shoulders, ran my hands down his legs, hoping that somehow it would help if he ached or was tired. I felt the old scars below his knees, the lines of the ropes that once tied him too tightly.

His ribs rose and fell.

"We'll sleep for a bit, Harry."

I tried really hard, but I couldn't *not* think of

the grey donkey with the bricks, fallen by the roadside. When I closed my eyes, when I opened them, he was there. Frank had said the grey donkey would have got up if he could. It was the man from Mumbai's fault he fell the first time. Now it was mine.

Harry wasn't asleep. His eyes were half open, his nostrils twitched a little. I could tell he was also watching me, although he didn't look me in the eye. I didn't know what I was looking for but it was what Frank had done. He watched him and watched him and then he seemed to know what to do.

Donkeys don't sleep much, I knew that, and they don't always lie down to sleep. If he needed to rest, then I'd just let him lie there. I stayed quiet and waited and watched Harry's eyelashes flicker. I tried to feel what he felt.

Harry moved his neck, so he could see me better, still without looking right at me. He breathed and disturbed the dust on the ground. His ears twitched, turning towards me, then away.

The sky was that kind of miracle deep blue, bright and cleaned for the night. Cool air dropped on to my shoulders.

Harry turned towards me as if he was checking I was still there. His ears swivelled. I really wanted to whisper into his tall ears, something nice, something good that would persuade him to keep going, to come home with me.

Harry raised his head and almost, *almost* looked me in the eye, and then lay back down, moving his head further away as if he was disappointed that I wasn't what he wanted to see. I wasn't sure that Frank was right about Harry choosing me instead of him.

"It's hard, Harry, but I want us to be cherries and almonds too, even if Frank's not here."

I rolled on to my knees and lay across his side, staying there for a while to feel him breathe. I wondered why Frank had said that pulling Harry up when he fell from the weight of the bricks had made things worse. Was this something Harry had to choose to do himself? I did the only thing I could think of. I reached over and gently smacked Harry's bum, and then I said what I did because that's all there was to say, "You know you can trust me, Harry. But I think you have to do this bit by yourself."

I didn't look back as I trudged home with my own heavy weight, hoping I'd done the right thing.

23.

WHEN I CAME ALONG THE TRACK, MARIANNE was sitting on the bench outside the guesthouse, and for a second I forgot that Frank wouldn't be there. Marianne leaped up, and then we just stood there for a minute looking at each other.

"Peter's gone home but he came here first and told me what happened." She looked different. I couldn't really say how, but I also was too afraid to look back, so I just went to her and we met in the middle. Her arms were warm and she smelled familiar and good and she bundled me right into her like I'd been gone for years.

"I'm sorry," she kept saying. And I knew that she was trying really hard to make up for something, for not really making me important like Frank had. Still holding me she whispered into my ear.

"It's me that needs to change, not you, not Frank. You're strong and sensitive, loving and so beautiful, and I don't know what I've been thinking all this time. I should never have let you go alone. What was I thinking? Perhaps I wasn't. You're still just my little girl. But I'm here now. Really here." She swept the hair away from my eyes.

"I didn't think you'd get it, why I had to go."

"I've got you now."

And then it was easy to tell her the words inside me.

"I left Harry by the roadside. He wouldn't come any further, and I had to leave him behind."

"It's OK, it's OK."

"It's what happened to Harry in Mumbai when Frank found him. Maybe he hadn't fallen down, maybe he just lay down because what he had to carry was too much for him."

"Not any more. He's got you. *And* he's got me. Together we'll rescue him. Even though we've never quite been a matching pair, not like… not like you and Frank, or Frank and Harry. Or you and Harry. We never quite fitted together because we were too different. I always gave you what *I* wanted. But it wasn't what you needed at all. That's why Frank thought you needed someone to stand by you for a while longer until you were ready, someone to give you what I didn't. I guess that's why he left Harry. The other half of him that could stay." She held me. "I've seen how you take care of Harry. I'm ready to take care of you now too. You should have had your mum with you all along."

We stood there for a long time, all her words melting into me.

"Hope?" she breathed, and when I looked up, she was pointing behind me.

Slow muffled hooves scuffed along the track. I turned around. I held on to my mother as Harry trudged towards the house. He stood there for a little while and that was the second time he looked me right in the eye. His ears and eyes turned towards my mother and my friend. He kept walking before stopping a short distance away from the bench, his nostrils flickering. His ears fell back and I knew it was because Frank wasn't there. Harry had chosen to get up, to come back, but maybe that was only because he thought he might still find Frank here?

My mother hesitated. I could see she was about to say something to me, then she shook it away as if something better needed to be said.

"Well done, Harry. You made it home." She told him.

Deep down inside, I was cheering for Harry, but had he really come back for me?

"It's not fair to make you or Harry do anything more than you already have," my mother said. She began collecting the things she needed to make a stable around Harry, just like Peter and I had the night before.

Marianne went into the house and brought out

a sleeping bag and cushions and blankets. She brought down my hammock and hung it on our porch.

"In you get," she said, helping me up as if I was wounded. She climbed in beside me, in the hammock that we'd brought with us when we first came here, where we'd lain together all night watching the mountain turn dark, drawing the outline between the stars with our fingers.

We swayed in the hammock, still in our clothes, her arms around me. She whispered lots of things about Canigou, about herself, as if she had only just realised that there might be a way that we fitted together perfectly.

"If I remember that night when we first came here and slept in the hammock..." she said, "when I remember that night, I want to start again from there."

We listened to the soft grind of Harry's teeth on the hay.

"It's all right that Harry's here with us, isn't it, Mum?" I whispered, as if I had to dare myself to ask.

"More than all right. This is a new beginning." I think she was crying, and that had nothing to do with Harry, and everything to do with me and her.

I slept in the hammock most of the next day with Mum watching over me and checking on me every five minutes. She didn't ask me to get up, she didn't go to her studio either. Peter came round and sat with me for a while and read one of his books out loud to me, a story his father had chosen for him. He told my mother that Nanu said to go over for coffee (which also probably meant a spread of food on the kitchen table), which was nice for my mother. Nanu had a soft spot for Mum, especially when Mum was alone.

In the evening, Harry came over to the hammock by himself, and I scratched his head and nuzzled against his nose and tried to believe that he wanted to be here.

He still wouldn't go in the shed though, so Mum and Peter made up the stall around him again, this time right next to the hammock.

And things went on like this for a while. Days went past but it was as if time stood still. I lay in the hammock, Peter came over and the only thing that was moving on was the story he read to me. Harry slept in his makeshift shelter. It felt easier just to push everything aside in this way and sleep.

And then one day, I don't know why, I knew something had to change. It had already changed in me and I needed Harry to see it too. Peter had put his book down, leaving it open, and it looked just like the roofs of the village. I thought about us still being halfway through a story. I thought about what I'd like to happen next.

Harry came up from the meadow and headed for the hammock. It was becoming a new habit for him, to come over for a cuddle, for me to say g'night, and him to wait for us to build the stall around him. This time I jumped down from the hammock with my blanket and went into his shed without looking back. I didn't really think what I was doing or why. It smelled a bit in the shed, but not awful like you'd expect. Kind of sweet and earthy and familiar. Harry's home. I shuffled straw into a bed for me and lay down and closed my eyes.

* * *

There was bright light on my eyelids, a new day, my mother whispering, "You did it!"

Harry had slept the night in the stable with me.

I thought about that time with Frank and the trailer and how I'd cheered, but Frank hadn't seemed as if it was the triumph it was. I think I knew why, now. No matter how brilliant it was that Harry had broken his old habit, when Harry chose to be with me instead, it meant Frank was closer to saying goodbye to him. That morning, it reminded me again that all the clever things that Harry had learned, were because Frank had left.

We did this for a few nights until Harry chose to go into the shed all by himself. Now I knew that even though he needed me, he could also rely on himself, too. That night I took my hammock back up to the roof, and slept there.

* * *

When I woke the next morning, I found a note from Peter: *When you feel ready, let's go over to Canigou. There's something I want to show you.*

My head was still kind of numb. I wasn't tired, not in that way you are when you've walked forever to get a stubborn donkey back home. More like I could only think of one thing at a time, kind of quietly, moving slowly to get showered and dressed while Marianne tried to help by making up a bag of things for me to take, checking with me what I needed.

"Do you want a spare T-shirt? You should take the sun cream. Do you want the after sun as well? Shall I put them both in? Will that make the bag too heavy?" Questions that seemed to float by me but that told me she only thought of me. I felt us drawing together, closer than we'd ever been. I nodded and said, "Whatever you think, Mum."

"Are you sure you want to go?" she asked. "I don't have to paint today, so why don't you stay at home and rest, let me look after you. You still look worn out, Hope. This will wait."

"It's not fair on Peter. He's not had any fun yet this summer."

"Hope," Marianne said as I was about to leave, "I'm sorry things turned out like this."

She looked smaller. Or had I grown taller?

She had changed. We all had. All of us except Frank who had gone back to the way he was, back on the road.

I let Harry out of the shed and led him down to the meadow.

He looked no sorrier for himself than he always did. Still the same shy eyes and drooping head. I wondered how his memory worked. Had he forgotten the last few days? Or did he still have the burden of what had happened, of Frank leaving us, weighing like bricks on his chest, like I did. I hoped he didn't, but it occurred to me for the first time that perhaps he had always been that way. That was probably the saddest thought I'd ever had: that sometimes sad things happen and then you're stuck like that forever.

"We'll be all right, Harry. We will. If I could have carried some of those bricks for you, I would've, just like Frank. If you've got any others left, though, you know, somewhere inside, I can carry them for you too."

I hoped the meadow would be all he thought of today, and all he felt would be the endless supply of sappy green grass and flowers, crunching between his teeth.

24.

Peter took one look at me and asked, "Are you ready?"

"When is anyone ever ready?" I said. "How do I know what I'm supposed to be ready for?"

"We could go another day," he said, but I wanted something new to think about.

"Let's just go."

Bruno grumbled at us in the lane. I had food for him and he was happier eating the leftover chicken I'd kept for him and letting us past than guarding us against going across the field, but I still hadn't found a way to make us good friends who properly understood each other yet.

It was another long walk before we reached the old shepherd's hut at the foot of the mountain. Part of the back wall and half the roof had crumbled where the avalanche had crushed it. Peter climbed through the wall and stood on the rubble. He gathered up a few of the stones and tried to stack them.

"You know, we could fix this up," he said. "It could be a really good place for Harry. He'd love it here."

"Maybe we'll bring him another day," I said.

A stone fell back out but Peter quickly picked

it up, turned it over, and found a better way to wedge it back in.

"We could clean it and make it nice," he said, trying to rebuild the wall. "Harry would be safe and dry, and maybe we could take the door off so he could go in and out whenever he wants."

"It's OK, he goes in the shed at night now."

Why it came into my head right then, I didn't know. But moments in the last few days suddenly seemed to tumble together, like I could almost make sense of them, but there were still things missing.

"Peter, remember that day at the waterfall? When you said you heard Frank and my mother talking and you knew Frank was leaving?"

I waited but Peter didn't reply.

"Why did you go there, Peter? We said we were going to meet at the waterfall. Why did you go to my house first?"

Peter dropped the stone, turned away. Why is it that the things that people don't say bother you the most?

"Peter?"

"I wanted to warn Frank…" he said, at last. "But then I saw Frank and heard he was leaving, and so I thought I didn't need to tell him any more."

"So whatever it is you can tell me because it doesn't matter now."

Peter picked up another stone and threw it at the wall, knocking down everything he'd just built.

"What didn't you tell him, Peter?"

"Frank should have taken Harry with him! He should have and then… and then…" He swung around. "Harry could live here, couldn't he? I mean, you can come up at the weekends. And when I'm here, we'll come together. In the holidays. Every day."

"Why would Harry need to live here, Peter?" My heart was beating fast, like I'd heard the crack of the snowdrift over on the mountain and it was about to fall, and I saw Peter take a deep breath to get ready to tell me.

"Because Papa is going to turn our meadow into a new vineyard because of what happened here with the avalanche, and Harry won't be able to stay with you any more."

"*Your* meadow?"

Peter held his head in his hands and sat on the ground, saying, "It's our meadow. It always was. That's why I came to see you that first day when Harry arrived. To tell you the meadow was ours. But Harry was in the meadow, and I really liked him, so I asked Nonno and he said it would be OK for Harry to use the meadow for a while, until Papa decided what he wanted to do with it."

I walked away from him, sank down in the grass, like an empty sack of nothing. Freshest, greenest meadow he'd ever seen in his life. And Harry wasn't even safe there.

Now it all made sense. Peter's enthusiasm about helping me put Harry and Frank back together was because of this. Peter was standing by his family. I closed my eyes from the sun, from the things I didn't want to see. Why did people keep hurting Harry?

"Why does your dad need the meadow now?" I asked, angry.

"For vines, because of the avalanche, I just told you that."

"But what I mean is, why *more* vines?"

"It's business," he said, looking away.

"Money, you mean," I said, something boiling in me. "How much *more* money do you need?"

"Don't, Hope."

"Well, it's true! You and your family have got everything." We both stood and faced each other. "Harry's going to have nothing and nobody and I won't have Harry with me, and you… and you? What will you have? More of everything!"

"Don't say that!" Peter's shoulders dropped.

"You have to tell him, Peter; make him see. This isn't right. Harry will have nothing if your dad takes the meadow. And neither will I. I don't want to lose Harry, and Harry... how will he survive over here on his own?"

"He's my *papa*," Peter said.

"And Harry… Harry's like my family too. And family means everything around here, doesn't it!"

I pushed him. "Especially if you're a Massimo!"

I pushed him again but he was ready for me.

"I can't help I'm a Massimo!" he shouted, standing in front of me holding my arms. I didn't think he was trying to stop me pushing him again; he was making sure I stayed there with him. "And I *have* tried to tell him! He said he'll let Harry use the casot and field." Quietly, he added, "For now."

Nothing on the outside ever stayed the same, but I held on to everything true I had inside. It didn't actually surprise me that Peter would have tried. I didn't blame Peter, either, and I wouldn't have given up our friendship for anything. I couldn't lose anyone else important in my life. But the Massimos had all the power around here and I couldn't stand the thought of Harry on the mountain by himself.

"I tried, really I did," Peter said. "But he won't listen to me." He let go of my arms. "And it doesn't make sense to him about you and Harry being cherries and almonds."

It stopped me in my tracks.

"You actually told him I said that?"

He nodded.

He did understand the order of me, and always had, and I didn't know why I'd never understood that before. But I knew I stood even less chance than Peter of persuading Peter's dad.

I thought of Harry lying down on the mountain road, ready to give up.

"I can't let Harry down," I whispered. "Not now. Not when I've made him keep going, for me."

"Then don't tell Papa he has to give up the meadow for a donkey. He won't understand that."

"But that's what I want him to do." I turned away.

Peter hooked his arm through mine, drew us back together, and we walked, me leaning against him.

"I do love Harry, Hope." He blushed.

"Not more than I do."

He smiled without looking up.

"You and Harry are the best pair."

"Like us, though?"

He nodded.

"Are you jealous?" I said.

His face flushed.

"No."

"You are."

He blushed again. "What flavours are we?"

I smiled. "You pick."

"Anchovies and olives."

"They're both the same though, strong and salty, and I don't even like anchovies."

"But I really do."

"So you'll be olives then."

He grinned. But this didn't change anything about the meadow.

"Remember Bruno?" Peter said, more serious. "Remember how he barked about the avalanche? And Harry, hee-hawing?"

I frowned. "You think I should bark or make noises like a donkey?"

He tried to disguise a smile. "No, although you're the kind of person to do something like that."

I couldn't help smiling back.

"What I mean is *you* could speak to Papa. Speak to him and say something that will make him understand."

I wondered, in the end, who Peter would stand by, and if I could let the words I wanted to say out in to the world. Or if Monsieur Massimo would want to hear them.

25.

My mother was walking down the drive to meet me when I got home, like she'd been waiting, looking out for me. I wanted to tell her about the meadow but before I had a chance to say anything she handed me a postcard.

"Go read it," she said. "I'll be in the studio. If you need me… for anything."

I went up to the roof terrace. I touched all the

things I kept in the curve of the roof tiles before I could look at it.

The word *Australia* was printed across the bottom.

So I knew where Frank was. He had gone home. I tried to find details in the photograph, something that told me more than that one word. There was sun, sand, waves, but nobody in the picture. A perfect beach. Empty. Did he feel like that too?

I turned it over and caught my breath. He'd always made me something for my birthday and Christmas, but never given me a card. The things I kept in the curves of the roof tiles were all the words he had needed to say. Pieces of wood left over from projects, that we'd look at and guess what they could be, that almost looked like what they would be even before he'd chiselled and sanded and worked at them. Hummingbird, the letter H, mermaid, donkey, cherries, knot. They all meant something at the time.

I hadn't seen Frank's writing before and, even though he'd gone, it felt like he'd invited me into another part of his world.

Seen my brother for the first time in twenty years.

Not staying long though. There's something else I got to do. Harry won't let you down.

Frank.

Short sentences, as if he'd had a whole heap of things to say but no room to talk about them. No love, not in words, but I saw the space he'd left around the words. I felt the room he'd always given me to think, to be me.

I read it again and again, until it seemed like

he'd written me a whole chapter of a book. A story we were both still in.

I ran down to the studio, calling my mother's name. She was painting and looked over her glasses and shoulder, as if for a moment she was going to warn me to leave her alone, which she was in the habit of doing when she was painting.

She hesitated. She'd always said that it had better be important if I disturbed her like that while she was working, but this was different and so was she. Immediately I was distracted from what I wanted to tell her when I saw what she was painting.

"It's me!"

She lay down her brush.

"I thought I'd... I wanted to try something new."

Even just with the wild strokes and simple

shapes she'd made so far, I could see the picture was of me asleep on her sofa. There were photographs of me pinned to her wall that she'd been copying.

"Don't say anything yet," she said, although I didn't know what to say anyway. It was too new to know how I felt.

"Is it for us?"

She wiped at some paint on her hands, scratching at a dried patch on her nail.

"I've got the real thing, why would I need a picture? You know, I don't remember my life, how it was before you. I was so busy trying to get everything to fit in with me that I hadn't thought about how *I* fitted into the whole picture. I think all along you've been my perfect other half." She laughed. "That sounds like the world according to Hope Malone. Actually –" she held out her hand to draw me over and we stood in front of me (*me!*) and stared – "I thought I might be able to get a buyer for this. I could get quite a lot of money for it if you agree we can sell it, as it's you after all." I looked into her eyes, waiting, because I knew she had so much for me right that minute, all the best in her.

"I suppose Peter has told you now about the meadow.

"You knew about the meadow already?"

"Nanu told me the other day, and I was going to tell you but Peter thought he should." Before I had chance to say anything else, she said, "We could use the money from selling the painting, see if we could buy the meadow from the Massimos for Harry."

My mother was different. Frank and Harry had changed us both in lots of ways, and we could only see it now Frank had gone.

"Who'd want a painting of me?"

She looked at the paint on her fingers. "Your father might."

"Would he?"

"Talk to me, Hope. You can, you know. If you want to."

Me? His daughter. Was I his daughter? What did it mean if there were these names for us but we weren't actually being these people. Maybe this was another storybook to open, but not now, not yet. Mum had said it as if she wasn't sure I would talk to her. Maybe I'd not given her a chance to understand me either.

"Yes, I do want to. But not today."

"When you're ready."

What I really wanted to know more about was her. Why had she painted me like this? Asleep. Lying on her sofa the day that Frank had left.

Shadows across the room, the sunset through the window behind, the soft glow of it over part of me, darkness over the rest of me.

"Why did you paint this picture?"

"Because I saw something about you that day that I'd never seen before. Often you don't notice something about a person that's there all the time, but then when you were asleep, I noticed it was gone. As if in your dreams you were free of... I didn't know what. And I realised that there's always been something you carry around with you that I've never quite been able to put my finger on, almost as if you were expecting something to be taken away from you at any minute." She swallowed, cleared her throat and steadied herself. "I'm sorry if there have been times when I didn't get the order of things right for you. I'm sorry if I didn't make you feel safe, if things didn't fit very well for you."

It made me think of Harry.

All along I'd not realised that the thing that had gotten to me the most about Harry was that he hadn't just fallen and been hurt that one day when Frank had crossed his path. Harry had been falling and falling and falling. And maybe Frank had realised it that one day. He wasn't like the tourists I'd met. He was a quiet sort of person who watched and watched, and he could see there was much more to a story than most of us do. He saw that it had been happening for a long time, again and again, and instead of pitying Harry, he set him free. But Harry must have been hurt so many times that he couldn't help being stuck with habits that he thought would make him safe. He only learned to break his habits because… because of me?

My mother led me over to the sofa and we held

each other as if we were two halves of just one person.

"What is it?" Mum said.

"What's a papa supposed to be like?"

"I don't know," she said. "I have no experience either."

"Shall I tell you?"

Even before I'd spoken she must have heard it coming.

"Frank," I said. She closed her eyes, nodding. "And you know why? Because he protected Harry and me all this time until we felt safe enough to grow by ourselves."

I leaned on her. "He brought Harry all the way across the world because he was looking for a place for Harry."

"Only at first."

"That means..." I thought for a minute. "That

means he always wanted to leave Harry with me, only I wasn't ready, either."

"Oh, Hope."

"Don't worry, Mum, I am ready now, but that's why we have to keep protecting Harry because he can't talk about all the things bothering him in his little donkey world, and we are going to have to figure it out for him."

We lay back and stared at the ceiling for a long time, both of us thinking. I wondered if one day my real father and I would want to try to see if we fitted together. How would I know if I never said those words to him?

"Frank is travelling because he's gone back to his old habits," I finally said, "but Harry and I – and you – we've learned some new ones."

"Which is pretty brilliant when you think about it," Mum said softly, tears on her face, like snow melting all at once. "What did Frank say on the postcard? I didn't read it. Somehow it seemed just for you."

"He said Harry wouldn't let me down."

She suddenly laughed through the tears and said it again as if it was true, like one of those things Madame tells you to make you behave thoughtfully. "Of course he won't! What a beautiful donkey Harry is." She kept laughing. "Still here, standing by you..."

"By us..."

"By us – no matter what happens to him. So loyal. Frank was right about him all along. Oh my God, Hope!" And in that second both of us sat forward. "Are you thinking what I'm thinking?" she gasped.

"My birthday!" I said because that's what had popped into my head right then as an answer.

"Your birthday? Oh, that wasn't what I was thinking, I thought I'd paint Harry and sell some—"

"Can we have my party here?"

"Here?" She sighed heavily, but not as if she was bothered, more like it was a big task she'd already resigned herself to facing. And I loved her for that. "But how does that help Harry?"

Dogs were barking in the village, and if you asked me right then what was going to happen next, I'd have said that only the mountain knew.

26.

The Massimos were also determined to throw the party.

Nanu wouldn't hear of it when I asked Peter to tell her that Mum and I wanted to organise it. It was only three days away and she'd planned the menu already, listing on her chubby fingers what she was going to cook. Nonno shrugged and threw up his hands. Food wasn't something he had any say in.

Peter dragged me out of their kitchen to say, "I'm not being rude, honest, Hope, but my parents want it to be special, what with me – us – becoming teenagers. You know what they're like."

"And Harry? Remember we said it would be his birthday too?"

"Yeah, I know, but anyway, Nanu's already asked everyone, and I mean everyone. Monsieur Albert, all the people who work in the vineyards and their families, everyone!"

I needed to start again because I'd gone about this the wrong way.

"All we have to do is get them to come to my house instead," I said.

"How are we going to do that?"

"Peter, do you want to help Harry or not?"

"Yes, of course, but—"

"I'm not asking you to choose me over your family, I promise. Just help me."

He smiled, and said, "OK," and we went back into the kitchen.

"Nanu, you're the best cook in the whole village." And I did mean it. "Isn't she Peter?"

Peter translated and Nanu smiled, ducked her head as if she was shy.

"Best in the whole Pyrenees," Peter said when I nudged him, nodding enthusiastically.

She flicked her tea towel towards us at the compliment.

"Marianne really, really wants to do it, but you know she's not very good at cooking. And also she's on her own right now."

Nanu's eyebrows turned up over her eyes. Frank flashed into my mind, the sharp feeling of him being gone, but I carried on. "She needs friends. We don't have any other family and she needs people around her. So would you please, please help her?"

Nanu waddled over and put her arms around me. She pinched my cheek and smiled.

"Did she understand?" I whispered to Peter.

"I understand," Nanu said.

"Nanu, we want to have the party at our house but please would you do the cooking for us?" I asked.

"Please, Nanu, it's what I want too," Peter said.

After a lot of Italian talk between them, which involved arms waving a lot, it was agreed.

I went home and told Marianne and she said, "Oh my God, Hope! Have we got enough chairs? Are there any left in the woodshed? Where are we going to have it? Outside? It'll have to be outside. Cutlery! We need more cutlery. I'd better ask Nanu. And napkins! Remind me to get napkins."

She turned into someone else when she was faced with organising things. A kind of lunatic wildcat, tearing about all hissy and troubled.

"Are they making a cake? Do we need a cake? Should I make it?" Then she grabbed my face and kissed me hard right on the lips, and said, "It's Harry's birthday too, yes?" and hurried off to look for chairs while I taught Harry something new.

27.

MARIANNE BEING AN ARTIST, I KNEW THE party would somehow end up involving paint, the thing she was most comfortable with. When I woke up on the morning of the big day and looked outside my window at the mountain that was always there, I also saw my mother asleep on the porch below, still in her apron, still with her glasses on. I was kind of happy, and I did feel safe with Canigou, Harry and Mum around me.

I went down to wake her and let Harry out. Harry nuzzled against me and I whispered into his long ear so that he'd know how sure I was that he wouldn't let me down.

"I trust you, Harry." He flicked his ears and turned and headed for the meadow. If my plan didn't work, it wouldn't be because of Harry.

Mum had put out two long tables in front of the house. Lying across the tabletops were two huge canvasses. She'd painted the most beautiful meadow filled with bright patches of wild flowers, Harry amongst them. They looked like her other paintings, but different too, almost like the movement you could see was the flowers actually growing. When I took the canvases off the tables, I saw she'd painted Harry on the tables too, vines growing around him.

By the time we'd laid the tables and stood back you could hardly see what was underneath, but we knew it was there and what this was all about.

"The vines are blue," I said.

"That's because—"

"I know, I know, you have to stop looking at the green to see the blue, or something. Like, without the blue, they wouldn't be green. I like it. I think I get you."

She laughed. "Exactly," and then insisted I put on a dress and brush my hair.

"You've always said I should wear what I feel comfortable in," I said, looking down at my dusty canvas shoes and old shorts.

"Yes, I know, but today is different."

"So we have to be different?"

"No, not who you are." She put her hands on her hips and sighed. "Just who you need to *appear* to be to the Massimos. We need to impress them today..."

"I like my old shorts. My shorts like me too."

"Think of it as a game. We're just disguising the things about us that Peter's father... well, doesn't understand. Make him think we think like him, I suppose."

"But we're not like him."

"I know, but we need to communicate the right message."

"And the message is that we're not the odd child and mad deranged mother that Peter's parents probably think we are."

She laughed. "Something like that."

I smiled. "I'll do it for Harry."

"So will I, because that means it's for you too."

It was only ten o'clock and the visitors weren't coming until noon, but I wiped my shoes, changed, itched in the dress bought by my mother for visiting galleries that I'd never worn (it was actually a bit small now and tight across my chest), breathed deeply and headed down to the meadow.

Mum called, "I nearly forgot! Happy Birthday, Hope! Happy Birthday, Harry!" Outside I smiled. It was actually Peter's birthday today, ours wasn't for another five days. Inside I handed everything that was about to happen over to Harry. And hoped.

It only took a couple of minutes for me and Harry to walk to the Massimos, but we smelled the food that was cooking long before we got there as it mingled with the smell of vines and earth and sun-baked ground.

The kitchen door was wide open, food already piled high in baskets and bowls, covered in red and white checked teacloths. Peter was waiting. He knew the plan. He smiled, crossed his fingers.

"I've come to help," I said to Nanu. She came straight over telling me how pretty I looked and I blushed at the same time as Peter.

"No, no," she said. "I take care of everything."

"There's too much for you to bring," I insisted. "Harry can carry some of the food over."

She blinked, suddenly noticing Harry in the doorway, two baskets strapped either side of the pads on his back. Peter looked at Nanu, and calmly said, "Good idea, Hope. Saves us a lot of trips."

"Harry loves to help," I said, wedging the bread inside Harry's baskets. "Shall I take the fruit?"

Nanu smiled. "Yes, OK, good donkey," she said.

I smacked Harry twice gently on the bum.

Nanu fed us olives and bread and oil and I was

careful not to let the crumbs fall on my clothes.

A few minutes later, I squeezed my lips tight. Catching Peter's eye, we grinned and grinned at each other because Harry was standing by the back door again, now with empty baskets. It's what I had taught Harry to do. There was a little note stuffed in the side of his harness. It was from my mother in her beautiful writing. It said, *You did it again! Xxxx*

"What else can he take?" I said.

Harry went up and down the lane by himself while Peter and I made sure everything was secure in the baskets. After Harry had made a few trips, Nanu left a pail of water and a carrot for him. She picked a lily from the bunch on her table and pushed it into Harry's harness. Harry was winning her over.

When nearly all the food had been taken up

to our house I noticed Nanu sizing Harry up, almost as if she was thinking she could get a lift to our house too. Nanu was very short, hardly taller than me, but she was very round all the way down, so I quickly said, "I'll just take the cheeses up and then Harry's got some things to do for my mother."

I tapped Harry's shoulder but first Peter and I went outside where Nonno had been sitting reading a paper.

"We're going up to Hope's," Peter said. "Do you want to walk with us?"

Nonno nodded and came with us. Nonno had suffered from polio when he was a boy. It made the bones in his legs short and curved and, as he'd got older, his hips were stiff because of the way he waddled. We slowed for him.

Harry was following us, but I stopped and went

back to him, hooking my arm over his neck so he would walk beside me. Peter moved out the way so that Nonno was on the other side of Harry.

Peter spoke to Nonno in Italian.

"Harry?" Nonno said.

"The donkey, Nonno."

"Ah, si. Harry." (I knew *si* meant yes.)

I was a bit uncomfortable that Nonno had seemed to forget who Harry was, but then I felt Nonno's arm against mine, Harry holding Nonno's weight against him, helping him up the track to our house.

Nonno didn't look back at Harry when he went to greet my mother. But Nonno had been there for us, or maybe for Peter, and I was sure he hadn't forgotten our journey to the airport. Surely it meant something to him. But he wasn't going to be the most important person to convince.

My mother invited Nonno to sit in the shade and called me over.

"This arrived."

Another postcard. A sand-coloured building with huge arches. Crowds of people. *Greetings from Mumbai.* I turned it over quickly.

Noisy here, not like the mountains. Seems a different world this time. Found a place to stay for a while. How's my girl?

Frank.

I read into all the details. He'd gone back to the place where he'd found Harry. I'd never thought of it before, that Harry might have interrupted Frank's travels, that it was still a place that he hadn't finished exploring and had only left there because he wanted to take Harry away.

How's my girl? His girl. Words that joined me to him still.

There was an address at the bottom.

I left the card in the hammock and would write back later, when I could tell him how today had ended.

28.

SOON PEOPLE FROM THE VILLAGE ARRIVED FOR the party. Loads of people, including Monsieur Albert and the Vilaros, and some children I knew from school whose parents worked for the Massimos.

Peter's father and mother came last, like the royal family, everyone fussing around them. Peter's father wore a suit. I didn't like that because it looked like he was at a business meeting and that wasn't exactly the kind of mood I hoped he'd be in. I'd never really had a conversation with him before. He was one of those people that made words get stuck inside me. I didn't ever think I had anything to say that he would want to hear anyway.

Peter's mother was the best-dressed person there and she didn't take off her black sunglasses the whole time.

There were gifts, mostly for Peter, some for me.

More chairs were brought out from inside.

I'd talk to Monsieur Massimo soon.

Peter's little cousins raced around Harry and I went over and told them, "You have to give Harry some time to get used to you." They looked up at me, and I liked that a lot, listening as if I had something important to say. Which I did. "He doesn't know you're going to be kind to him yet, even though I do."

They giggled and became more gentle, asking if they could feed him apples and carrots, and I said, "Not too many, but you can brush him if you like."

While they were doing that, Peter and I stood the two huge canvases up to make a backdrop for a stage. Peter invited all his little cousins to sit down and stood on our stage with me.

"It's Peter's birthday," I said. "Shall we sing happy birthday?"

The children sang and clapped and the adults gathered around.

"Harry knows it's Peter's birthday," I said. I called Harry where he was waiting behind the screens. "Do you have something for Peter, Harry?"

I clapped my hands twice.

Harry appeared and went straight to Peter, one basket stuffed with sweets for the children who ran to him, eager to be part of what was going on. The other basket had my present to Peter. He opened it and blushed when he saw I'd given him the carved olive knot handle, now fixed on top of a walking stick.

The children asked, "What's that for?"

"It's for when we're ninety-nine," Peter said, with a big smile.

"It's also Hope's birthday soon," he said. "We're celebrating Hope and Harry's birthdays today."

He started to sing with the children and their voices were beautiful, even more so when they sang for Harry.

Peter's father walked towards us. My hands were sweaty, my throat dry. I'd just wait a minute and then speak to him.

"This is for you," he said to Peter. He'd bought him a watch.

Peter's father had a serious voice that made people listen, and when he'd spoken everyone went quiet so I thought I'd wait a minute longer before I asked him about the meadow.

"I also have a surprise for my son." Everyone was listening as Peter's father continued.

He turned Peter around, led him to one side of the canvas screens, and the children went running over asking, *What is it? What is it?*

Peter's father pointed to the meadow and said to us all, "As you know, we lost the vines under the avalanche a few months ago. But there's no turning back, the future is important. So I've decided to turn this meadow into a vineyard."

I felt panicky inside and wished he'd stop talking so I could speak to him first, but I never got a chance to say the words, to let them out into the world to try to change his mind. It had already been decided, already been announced to everyone, and I hadn't thought of that. Without saying anything, I knew Harry and I didn't stand a chance against all the people who would want the new vineyard.

Then Monsieur Massimo looked down at his son.

"We're going to name it Peter's vineyard, and when you are twenty-one, Peter, it will be yours to run as you choose."

Peter turned to look at me. I could tell he had no idea that his father was going to do this.

I couldn't listen any more, the words inside me buried under feeling hopeless. I backed away from all of them, from Peter who was mouthing sorry at me, from my mother who had something in her hands she was trying to give to me. From all the people in the village who would earn money and have work, who needed and wanted the new vineyard that meant more than a donkey ever could.

I walked into something, stumbled.

"Hope!" Peter called.

And I wished he hadn't. Everyone looked as I tripped over Harry.

Harry didn't look me in the eye and I couldn't stand for him to see how sorry I looked for myself. Did he know what I'd done to him? Because it was my fault. Frank had left Harry behind for me, so I could keep him safe. It was also Frank's way of saying, *Hold on to this important part of me and take care of it.* But I hadn't.

I couldn't look Harry in the eye. He didn't know that I'd be leaving him alone in the empty casot on the mountainside.

29.

HARRY HAD A FEW WEEKS LEFT TO EAT THE meadow before the Massimos asked the Vilaros to turn over the soil, bang in stakes and wire them up, before planting the new vines in early winter. Harry didn't know a thing about time, and munched and wandered through the grass and flowers like it would never end. I remembered what that was like, not knowing what was going to change or how big the changes would be, how two things that seemed to fit perfectly together, like Harry and the meadow, would not be able to any more. Maybe I was wrong about these things all along.

I wasn't angry with Peter about what happened. What can you do when one family is stronger than another?

My mother came up to the roof terrace later that day. She had always given me room to do what I wanted, but this time I felt her on the edge of my space, maybe making sure she didn't give me too much room, just enough.

"Frank left this for you, for your birthday," she said, holding out something the size of a tennis ball, wrapped in paper. "Actually he said it was for both you and Harry, but I suppose you had better open it or Harry might eat it."

She smiled, trying to lift me up.

Inside the wrapper was a globe carved from wood. I nearly dropped it, the two halves coming apart in my hands. I looked closer at the map of the world carved into each half of it. At the two crosses marking the names of the places.

"France and Mumbai," I said. "Look how far apart these places are. Where I am, where Frank is. Look how far Harry had to come to be here with me and now—"

"Look how far you and Harry have come together," Mum said, "without having gone anywhere at all."

What Peter and I felt about Harry was much stronger than our differences, and our summer project became getting Harry used to his new home. Peter said sorry a thousand times, promised when he was twenty-one that he'd give the meadow to me and Harry. We both knew that would be too late, that it wouldn't ever really happen.

Every day we walked Harry over to the casot to let him graze there and get used to it, and we piled the stone wall back up as best we could. We'd wander off and leave Harry for a little longer each day and then we'd go inside the casot early evening to sit with him for a while. But I brought him home to his shed every night. It was our new habit. Our legs grew strong with walking.

Peter tried extra hard to make me laugh, but laughing was something I had gotten out of the habit of doing. We'd come back home and sit in the hammock and he'd read until I fell asleep.

"Sleep, if you need to," Mum said. "It's when all the things inside you can repair."

Sleep and I were getting to be good friends.

One day, Peter told me his papa wanted to talk to me.

"The grapes will be ready for picking soon and maybe your donkey could work in the vineyards. He'd be very useful. Peter tells me he likes to work."

Monsieur Massimo offered me some money to keep Harry in hay over winter.

I said, "All the money Harry ever needed was spent on him one time by Frank. To bring him here."

"I see," he said, but I wasn't sure he did.

"I think it's a good idea, Hope," Peter said. "Harry will work hard."

Monsieur Massimo held out his hand and I shook it. It was a business deal, after all.

* * *

September. Peter went back to boarding school in England. Mum hung up the painting of me in her studio. She painted the wall white again first, to make it clean, like we were starting again from somewhere new and bright. She told me my father had wanted the painting, but I said I wasn't ready to let him have it yet. She said we'd keep it close by for now, to remind ourselves of the things about us we loved, the things we couldn't always see. Together my mother and I made something more together, kind of more Marianne and Hope Malone.

When I went back to school, Mum bought me a mountain bike.

On my way to school, I'd cycle past Bruno, Harry trotting behind. Bruno didn't know what to make of my bike. He'd wag his tail and drool and sometimes run after us. He didn't bark any more though. Harry followed me to school and I let him. He had nowhere else to go while the meadow was being prepared and I didn't think either of us was ready for him to be on his own all day. I knew it would take a while to help him break the habit of wanting to be with me, so I thought being nearby was better. He'd wait outside the schoolyard, munching at geraniums in pots and the grass in the square nearby after he'd finished the hay that I'd brought for him. Then I'd cycle over to the casot with him after school, and leave him for a while. That was OK for a few days. But then villagers complained that their flowers had been eaten and also that socks had gone missing off their washing lines (which wasn't good for Harry at all), and then Madame called Mum in to ask us to keep Harry away.

I imagined these circles. Villagers in the middle, the Massimos right at the centre of everything that happened. People like my mother and me were in another outside circle, and then right outside was Harry. We could all pass through each other's circles, but we'd always end up in the same place.

At the weekend, I taught Harry what I wanted him to do on Monday.

Gently I taught him that tapping his right shoulder twice meant he had to go to the casot. Wherever we were. Slowly, he learned that he could follow me to school, and that when we got there, he had to walk to the casot by himself.

Of course, Harry didn't let me down.

Each morning Mum packed me snacks and drinks and anything I might need for Harry, so that after school I could cycle to be with him.

Soon he had work in the vineyards and I could leave him with the grape-pickers. I gave the money that Harry earned to old Monsieur Dubois the carpenter, to make alterations to the casot, to protect Harry from winter, which wasn't so far away. I always brought him back to the shed by the house at night though. I couldn't sleep if he wasn't there.

I loved that it was me Harry belonged to, as if I had also kept part of Frank that way.

After they had finished grape picking, Harry got another job carrying stakes for the workers in the new vineyard. He didn't seem to recognise that it was once his meadow. Maybe, like me, he had no choice but to give it up. As long as he had work some days he stayed quiet, and he was as sweet and gentle as ever.

I wrote to Frank every week, told him about Harry, about me.

He only wrote once more.

Mumbai has changed a lot. Frank

I wondered how a big city could change, I wondered if Frank ever would, but I guessed he'd moved on and my letters were in a pile behind some door. I sent more letters to him anyway, imagining that the growing mountain of words that he didn't read was marking the spot where something had to be left behind, like the Massimo's vineyard that got buried under the snow.

Everything changes. Frank told me that. All the seasons, and even people, which meant we had to move on, like the grooves in the bark of the tree where the swing used to be.

Up on the roof terrace one morning with Mum, I said, "I think only Canigou has stayed the same."

She said, "Maybe it's just moving slower than the rest of us."

I liked that she said that. I wondered if she felt the mountain breathing slowly, very slowly, holding things the steadiest they could be.

She watched that mountain for so long that I thought perhaps *she* had words inside her that needed to come out.

"Frank always said 'Spill' when he knew I was thinking about all sorts of things and… and I've only just realised, but I think he said it because he really did want me to share things with him," I said.

"I'm happy to share anything with you." She laughed. "Remember back in June, the Canigou flame?"

"When they lit the bonfires all across the top of the mountains?"

"Yes. In the morning, you could just see the red glow from the embers left there. Like a cherry on top of a cake." She laughed again. "It reminds me of you."

Peter came back for holidays. We were like we'd always been, together, only some days we'd both choose our own things to do, and that was OK. He went skiing with his father while I wandered around the village looking for lonely dogs. I fed them sausages, scratched their heads and whispered things in their floppy ears. Bruno still paced around the Vilaros' land, guarding the gate and wall of their field, but he got into the habit of following me too. That was OK with me because it made me think of Frank and how people sometimes just have to do things they can't help doing, even if wasn't OK with the Vilaros that Bruno kept doing a bunk.

While the winter snow still glittered on Canigou, Madame Vilaro came to see me. She asked if she could borrow Harry to help her collect and carry things from their land. Their field and wild woodland (the shortcut to the casot), which Bruno was supposed to be guarding, didn't have rows of fruit trees like everywhere else. It was sort of scrubby and woody.

"What are you collecting?" I asked.

"Truffles," she said.

So that's what Bruno had been guarding. The expensive knobbly blackish things that people like the Massimos ate, grew in the soil beneath the trees. I liked Madame Vilaro very much for asking. Truffles were hard to find but they didn't weigh much. She didn't really need Harry to carry them for her.

I asked her why she thought of Harry.

"Peter Massimo asked me," she said. And I knew Frank had always been right about him, that he would be kind to Harry.

"Bruno's not so good at guarding the truffles any more," I said.

Madame Vilaro said, "What can I do with a crazy dog like that?"

I shrugged. I was getting to quite like Bruno.

"Maybe he needs a friend," I said. "Then he'd be happier staying put."

30.

SPRING. THE CHERRY TREES BLOSSOMED, AND early one Saturday morning when I let Harry out of the shed and was about to take him over to the casot, I heard a dog barking in the village, a bark I didn't recognise. Kind of hoarse and yelpy.

I stuffed my pockets with everything I might need and asked Harry to come with me.

It was still early as we walked into the village. Coffee and fresh bread smells filled the air, but very few people were about.

Harry seemed to know better than me where the sound was coming from as we walked through the centre of the village. We stopped and listened. Harry turned towards Rue St Pierre, a cobbled alleyway off the square, and we looked down there before hearing the bark again. On the next road further along, we found the dog.

I didn't recognise her. She had three legs, the back left one missing right from the top. She was kind of like a hound, with drooping ears, a long nose and amber eyes. Her fur was mottled with darker brown spots. I suspected if she'd had a bath she would have actually been much paler.

Harry's skinny tail swished and his ears went up when the dog looked towards us. The dog had no collar and was sniffing around doorsteps. She shied away from us.

"Don't worry, Harry. She doesn't know we're going to be kind to her yet."

We followed her for a bit, Harry snatching at the verges and the bushes while the dog kept looking back at us. I had some sausage and half my croissant from home. When I unwrapped them, the dog sniffed the air. I broke off some chunks and threw them closer to her. She walked slowly over, nose to the ground, holding herself quite low, her eyes still watching me.

She snatched up the sausage, hopped back a little as if she was afraid I might try to take the sausage away again, as if her three legs might not be fast enough to get away if she needed to.

I liked her straight away.

"You're just perfect," I said. "Isn't she, Harry? Not for us though."

I turned and walked away, throwing more sausage behind me, Harry trotting by my side. Eventually we came out at Rue Allieri where there was a bench, and I sat down. Harry wandered over to the grass and the dog watched me from a distance.

Bruno, the wandering guard dog, popped out of nowhere like he usually did now, every time I was around.

I had no idea if the dogs already knew each other. They circled around each other for a bit, sniffing each other, tails held high. There were hackles and growls when I threw more food. Harry moved away. The dogs didn't seem that interested in him though, excited as they were to meet and share the sausage.

Harry was looking down the valley, nose twitching, and he seemed to want to go, so I walked beside him, my arm around his neck to spend some time with him at the casot. I looked back at the new dog, her ears up, watching us go.

"We'll take it slowly with her, Harry," I whispered into his ear. "But I think Bruno is going to be kind to her, don't you?"

Harry seemed to be in a hurry.

"OK, I'm coming," I said, running to catch up.

Bruno followed us down the track to Madame Vilaro's land, to the old kennel where he slept. As I walked away, trying to keep up with Harry, Bruno barked and howled at me. Probably wanting more croissant, I thought.

"All gone, Bruno." I turned back to show him my empty pockets and saw, coming down the lane, slowly and shyly, the three-legged dog. Bruno wasn't talking to me at all. Sometimes a dog knows what's what right away. I watched while they greeted each other again and wondered if she'd stay, and decided to bring them a blanket to sleep on tomorrow.

"We should give you a name," I said.

"Bruno and…" I thought for a minute. "Bruno and... Sylvie."

I'd heard that somewhere before, but I couldn't remember where. Probably in one of those books that Peter read.

I was happy that they had each other. That made complete sense to me.

"Bruno and Sylvie," I said again. "I think they might both be good guard dogs if they've got each other, don't you, Harry?"

But Harry wasn't beside me. He was trotting

down the lane, picking up speed, bony legs and tail flicking.

Dust flowers bloomed along the track, kicked up by a jeep and trailer coming our way.

I'd only ever seen Harry run like that once before, and the distance between him and the jeep closed in seconds.

I saw Frank through the dusty windscreen. And I was running to him too.

It was as if I'd been out for another day of adventure and come home and here he was. Like he'd been here just a minute ago.

He was out of the jeep, his arms open, and there wasn't anything to say because you don't need to when you have everything you want.

"How's my girl?" he whispered, not letting go.

I still had no word for what Frank was to me, but I felt it like a mixture of what I felt for my mother, and my friend Peter, and my other half, Harry.

"Thought I'd visit for a while, if that's OK with you?" he said.

Of course the answer was, "Yes, yes! Always."

Harry was kicking at the door of the trailer. I felt the sharp sting of Harry wanting to get back in the trailer so he could go travelling with Frank again. Until I heard something else. A donkey braying. Inside the trailer.

I looked to Frank for answers and he said, "There's a bit more to Harry's story. I didn't think you were ready to hear before."

Harry breathed through the thin gap in the trailer door.

"Who's in there?" I said.

"Donkey's aren't stubborn, Harry least of all," Frank said, as he opened the lock. "People think that, but I guess it's just that donkeys need to make sure they're safe before they trust people, and they take their time to think things over. They know who they belong with too. And they're loyal until the end."

Harry stood back and let Frank open the trailer door.

When the trailer door opened, it was just like that moment when Frank and I had seen the sudden breeze turning the blossom into pink snow on the mountainside. It's when your heart is the biggest it can be, because you're sharing it with someone you love. Inside Frank's new trailer was another donkey. Harry quivered and shivered all the way through his skin and bones and barrel belly when he saw that other dusty grey donkey.

Ever since I'd known him, Harry had seemed as if he'd still been carrying the bricks from years ago, but the way he trotted into that trailer and nuzzled up against the other donkey, he was as light and fluttery as cherry blossom petals.

It didn't feel like my mouth saying it, but the words, "Were there two of them in Mumbai?" came out as all the old reasons for Harry wanting to go back in the trailer, to stay with Frank, suddenly made sense.

"This is the grey donkey, Hope. He worked with Harry. Took me a while but I found him again, still carrying bricks, but at another building site in Mumbai," Frank said. "I'd seen them before, struggling, you know, when our paths crossed." There was no need to say what we already knew about them. "They both fell down that day, too many bricks, a building project that had to be finished quickly. It was Harry I pulled up. The grey donkey got up by himself."

At last I saw triumph in the way Frank looked at the two donkeys.

"You should have seen those two together, the grey donkey nudging at Harry to get up." I felt that weight again, of poor old Harry and how much he tried, how hard he tried, and didn't want to fail.

"The man would only sell me one. Harry was the oldest and the man thought he was the weakest because I'd helped him."

I held my hand out to the grey donkey and wanted to fall in love with him straight away.

"Frank? Did Harry want to go in the trailer all those years because he wanted you to take him back to his...?" Another word I didn't know.

Frank nodded as if he knew too that there are

some things that you can only feel but can't say. That maybe nothing ever really belongs to you, even if it feels like the other half of you.

"I think he'd rather have stayed on the building site than be without his friend," Frank said.

I made it worse. At last I understood those words.

"Even in the freshest, greenest meadow Harry had ever seen in his life," I said.

"All along Harry wanted me to take him back but it took me a while to work it out. Maybe something you said about cherries and almonds."

"You waited so long, Harry. So long."

"I figured he needed someone to take the place of the grey donkey. That was you, Hope."

Frank closed the trailer on the two donkeys and I understood why he'd found it hard to be happy about giving Harry his freedom. He'd set him free from one thing but that had also meant separating him from another.

Sometimes, you just suddenly realise that your life is just like a story, that you're only ever turning the page to a new chapter.

In the end I said, "Frank, did you miss us?"

He put his arm around me and left one of his big soft friendly silences for me to fill in. Of course he did.

"Thing is, it also took me a while to work out that taking Harry away wasn't any kind of answer. What about all the other donkeys? What about all the men who have families to feed and rely on their donkey to earn a living?"

I looked up at him. There was a whole bigger story, a wide, wide circle that affected so many people. And Frank gave me a heap of space while I thought about it some more.

"Hop in," Frank said, opening the jeep door.

"Where are we going?"

"Not far."

I got in the jeep and started to tell him on the way home about what had happened with the meadow, when he leaned across and opened the glove compartment. I saw the pile of letters I had written stacked neatly in there. Frank never was one for writing.

"I know, I read your letters. That's not where we're going. Peter Massimo also wrote to me a couple of times. His father has a patch of land he's willing to sell and a little old stone building at the foot of Canigou." He grinned. "Couldn't risk planting there, just in case that old mountain decided to throw an avalanche at him again."

"I love our mountain, Frank. Is that daft when you can't be sure it loves you back?"

"How can you be sure it doesn't?"

So many things to think about when Frank was around.

"You remember Bruno?" I said. "We get on quite well now, not best buddies exactly, but I found him a friend and I think they're going to be cherries and almonds too. I hope so. Well, anyway, Bruno had always been my friend only he wasn't really good at showing it. That time with the avalanche, I think he was trying to guard Peter and me."

"Good old Bruno."

We laughed and I thought Frank and I would probably remember Bruno when we were ninety-nine because of this.

We bumped along in the jeep, and I peered through the narrow glass window into the trailer. Harry and the grey donkey were pressed against each other, nibbling at each other's necks, rattling behind us with a bunch of carrots that they weren't the slightest bit interested in.

"What shall we call him, Frank? What goes with Harry?"

"Harry *and* Hope. We've got some time to think about it."

"You're still going travelling again, aren't you Frank?"

"Few weeks off first, rest a bit, see old Harry and the mountain. Spend some time with my girl."

I saw the future, blooming like cherry trees. Frank looked across and we were just like we'd always been.

"Spill," he said.

"Do you think one day maybe you could live out there, Frank? In Mumbai, I mean. Find a casot or an old tumbled down place you could do up? And a field or a meadow and some land? Do you think there's a place where all the old donkeys and the lonely ones could go and have someone who cares about them? Someone to help put cherries and almonds together?"

He nodded to himself. We had plenty of time to think.

"Did you know that cherries and almonds are related?" he said.

"They are?"

"Same family of trees."

I thought that of all the funny and brilliant things I'd ever heard, this was the best.

"Do you think, Frank, when I'm, say, eighteen, I could go out to Mumbai too? I mean, I'd like a job like that one day. I'd be like Harry then, having something useful to do."

He laughed, put his hat on my head.

"Five years' time? That's a long time for you to want something."

"Harry waited nearly five years to be together with the grey donkey again."

The jeep bumped us along the track.

"I'm a bit like Harry, aren't I, Frank?"

Dust spat up behind us.

Acknowledgments

Harry and Hope first appeared as a strong image in my mind after I was very late to an event. I hated having let the children down, and hoped that I could find a way to make up for it. It was on my way home from this event, trying to resolve my feelings, that the characters suddenly emerged. With some help from very generous people, the story developed.

My thanks to Jenna Goldby at The Donkey Sanctuary in Sidmouth who showed me how to train a donkey (I loved that!) and introduced me to Suchitra from the international team in India; and to Bob and Mavis Secrett, old family friends, who surprised me with an invitation to visit them in France.

Thank you Rachel Denwood, my editor, for your clarity and genius suggestion, as well as Sam Swinnerton and Lily Morgan who brought it all together. A special thanks to Sam White and the publicity team, who organise great events for me to attend and share the stories.

I am grateful to all the HarperCollins team and Julia Churchill, my agent, for everything they do, and to the children who read my books, even when I am late, so that I am able to continue my dream job.

My name is Cally Louise Fisher
and I haven't spoken for thirty-one days.
Talking doesn't always make things happen,
however much you want it to.

Cally saw her mum, bright and real and alive. But no one believes her, so Cally stopped talking. Now a mysterious grey wolfhound has started following her everywhere. Perhaps he knows that Cally was telling the truth…

Sometimes when things are broken
you can't fix them on your own –
no matter how hard you try.

When Nell is sent to stay with distant family, she packs a suitcase full of secrets. A chance encounter with a wild horse draws Nell to Angel – a mysterious, troubled girl who is hiding secrets of her own. Both girls must learn to trust each other, if they are to save a hundred horses…

Memories scoop you up and take you back to another time, so you can feel things all over again. I think of how important it is for all of us, but especially for Grandad, to remember the bright things from the past. But now he's forgotten everything and he hasn't told me his most important memory yet – the one about a whale...

Can Hannah piece together the extraordinary story that connects Grandad's childhood to her own?

Leo dreams about being a hero. In his imagination he is a fearsome gladiator, but he wants to be a hero in real life.

When the boys at school dare Leo to do something he knows is wrong, he lets everybody down. How can he make things right again?

A little dog called Jack Pepper is missing and it will take a true hero to find him and bring him home…